M000030899

Dear Romance Reader,

Welcome to a world of breathtaking passion and never-ending romance.
Welcome to *Precious Gem Romances*.

It is our pleasure to present *Precious Gem Romances*, a wonderful new line of romance books by some of America's best-loved authors. Let these thrilling historical and contemporary romances sweep you away to far-off times and places in stories that will dazzle your senses and melt your heart.

Sparkling with joy, laughter, and love, each *Precious Gem Romance* glows with all the passion and excitement you expect from the very best in romance. Offered at a great affordable price, these books are an irresistible value—and an essential addition to your romance collection. Tender love stories you will want to read again and again, *Precious Gem Romances* are books you will treasure forever.

Look for fabulous new *Precious Gem Romances* each month—available only at Wal★Mart.

Kate Duffy
Editorial Director

WEEKEND IN PARADISE

Suzanne McMinn

Zebra Books
Kensington Publishing Corp.

http://www.zebrabooks.com

With thanks to author Sylvie Kurtz and airline pilot Don Schramski for generously sharing their aviation know-how with me. Any mistakes are my own.

Chapter One

There she was.

Brade Cox watched strappy sandals topped by shapely calves and trim thighs emerge from a yellow taxi, followed by the rest of Dagmar Parker's lush body.

The business suit she wore was short, confident, sassy. Sexy.

He was aware of that fact, even from a distance, but he was a pro at separating his mind from the baser instincts of his body. He wasn't worried, but she should be.

She'd arrived on time, just as scheduled. It was almost too easy.

Not even a challenge.

Evidently she didn't suspect a thing.

From his position in the cockpit, Brade smiled to himself as he watched the interior designer cross the sizzling tarmac of Fortin Airfield toward his twin-engine craft, her curvy form silhouetted against the bright summer day. He'd never met her before, but Coop had shown him a couple of pictures.

She was even prettier in real life—she looked more like a model than a decorator. And just as he'd hoped, she was walking straight into his trap.

She was going to be angry when she found out that his grandfather, Leander Cox, would not be waiting for her on Half Moon Island. And she'd be even angrier when she realized that there was no house for her to decorate at all. The island was wild, a jungle rimmed by perfect beaches.

He loved it. She'd hate it.

But Brade wasn't the least bit concerned about Dagmar Parker's feelings. It was Coop he cared about.

Cooper Landon had been his best friend since grade school, and they'd remained close through college and afterward. Coop had been there for Brade when he'd needed him five years ago, and this was Brade's chance to pay him back. No way was he going to let Dagmar ruin Coop's chance at happiness—and with the way the flaky design consultant kept popping up everywhere from the bride's shower to the rehearsal tea, Coop was afraid the next place she'd turn up was the church.

Brade wasn't letting that happen, even if it meant he had to miss the nuptials himself. He'd been slated as best man, but he didn't mind stepping aside. Weddings made him uncomfortable, even Coop's. They brought back memories he didn't want to face.

Besides, he could use a vacation. He worked hard. Too hard, his family told him often enough even though it was the family business he worked in. A weekend away on secluded Half Moon Island, his wealthy grandfather's tiny private island off the South Carolina coast, wouldn't hurt him.

It wouldn't hurt Dagmar Parker, either. In fact, it might be just what she needed, even though she didn't know it yet.

Brade smiled to himself as he stepped out of the plane to greet his unsuspecting guest.

Melissa Reynolds opened her eyes, nervously peering downward as the small plane swept over the glistening, near blindingly bright Atlantic. Half Moon Island was a breathtaking contrast below, with its thick, dark, tropical-looking interior fringed by flawless white beaches.

A dizzy nausea had her closing her eyes again. Air travel did her in every time, without fail, and she fought to control the paralzying anxiety that came with it.

She took a deep breath and focused her thoughts on the beauty of the island view, playing back a mental picture of what the scene evoked—just the way she'd read in a self-help book on overcoming fears.

Days of sun-filled relaxation came to mind instantly—a result of overwork, she figured. But a vacation was only a fantasy. Number one, she had no money, and number two, she had no time.

And number three, she had no one to vacation with. Well, there was Dagmar, sure. But this island paradise made Melissa long for a more romantic holiday than that, which surprised her, since she was normally quite sensible about romance and its place—or lack thereof—in her life.

Maybe someday. For now, she had a job to do.

"It's beautiful," she shouted over the engine noise, daring to open her eyes and look over at the pilot. She kept her gaze carefully off the view outside the plane. If she could just pretend they were sitting in a little room on the ground. . . .

The pilot's serious profile didn't change, which annoyed her. He didn't have to be so rude!

The man had barely spoken to her since he'd met her on the tarmac of Fortin Airfield. He'd looked her over with a disconcerting gaze, his eyes shielded by dark sunglasses. He'd appeared to take in every detail, then he'd escorted her into the plane and promptly behaved as if she didn't exist.

She had no idea why she was letting him bother her. He wasn't the one she was here to impress. She was here to impress toy manufacturing mogul Leander Cox, and this man—Brade, as he'd so pithily introduced himself—was nothing more than the way to get her there.

Brade-with-no-last-name was handsome, in a dangerous sort of way. Thick black hair, dark tanned skin, devastatingly hard body.

Dagmar would like him, Melissa couldn't help thinking to herself.

He was rough, risky, and all too masculine. Melissa didn't have to know a single thing about Brade, not even his last name, to know that he was a heartbreaker, and Dagmar had a fatal attraction for the type.

Not Melissa. She was too sane, too smart, too practical.

And as long as she and Dagmar were going to run a design business together, somebody had to be practical—and it wasn't going to be her flighty cousin. Melissa might have fleeting daydreams about romantic fantasy holidays, but she knew they had no place in the here and now. Not for her.

Melissa was the business head, managing the marketing, accounting and other organizational details of Carolina Chic while Dagmar was the creative dreamer who came up with the designs. Their partnership worked . . . most of the time.

Today was an example of one of those times when the partnership worked better for Dagmar than it did for Melissa.

She should never have agreed to today's farce. Never. But Dagmar had been in tears. She had to see

Cooper Landon one more time, and it had to be today—because tomorrow her ex-flame was getting married.

Melissa could only hope that if Dagmar was rejected one more time by Cooper, she would finally face facts. She was trying to be gentle and understanding, but her cousin's penchant for romantic melodramas was wearing on her nerves.

They'd invested every penny they could scrape together in their struggling interior design business, Carolina Chic. They'd even had their own fabrics produced, to suit their unique decorating style of subtle watercolors and minimal furnishings, all perfectly suited to beach living along the Carolina coast.

They'd done homes of friends at cost and paid for expensive photography to showcase their ideas—and they'd spent the past year subsisting on peanut butter and crackers and juggling creditors while they built up a sporadic clientele.

Finally, *finally,* word of mouth was bringing in clients. They actually had appointments coming in—from paying customers, not friends—and Melissa had even secured a small, but important, photo spread on one of the homes they'd decorated coming up in the next *Southern Sophisticate* magazine.

And just when things were coming together for their business, Dagmar's romantic-crisis-of-the-month was turning into the romantic-crisis-of-the-day.

Melissa knew better than anyone why Dagmar was so hungry for love. Neither of them had grown up with much of it in their lives. Her cousin reacted by searching for it desperately, while Melissa shied away from it. But even though they had completely different ways of dealing with the past, Melissa's heart responded to Dagmar's pain.

Melissa was tough when it came to business, but she was a marshmallow when it came to Dagmar—and unfortunately for Melissa, Dagmar knew it.

So here she was, taking Dagmar's place and feeling unutterably foolish about the deception. But Melissa herself had taken the call from Leander Cox's assistant. He'd left no room for error—they were specifically requesting Dagmar, whose creative flair Cox's assistant said the toy tycoon had heard about through "friends of friends." And with the interior design of a 25,000-square foot luxury beach home on the line, Melissa'd had no choice but to ensure the job for Carolina Chic.

She'd read enough about the eccentric magnate to know that if they wanted the job, they'd better go along with the old man's wishes. Even if it meant that not only did she have to pretend to be Dagmar, she had to get on a plane—something she usually avoided at all cost.

Melissa's stomach dipped uncomfortably as the small plane circled and began its descent. Landings. She hated landings the most. Even more than take-offs. Squeezing her eyes shut again, she tried to focus on the meeting she would be having very soon with Leander Cox.

She had to be in control, strong, successful. .   Or at least, she had to project all of those things.

The fact that she was here to begin with—taking Dagmar's place, ready to kowtow to a wealthy client they desperately needed—made it all too apparent, to herself if not to anyone else, that she wasn't quite *there* yet in reality.

But she was working on it. And she was good at faking bravado. She'd been doing it most of her life.

She felt the plane continue circling and flicked her eyes open for a nauseating, desperate second to see the plane zoom over the water and head straight toward a landing strip cut into a grassy area between the beach and the interior jungle.

Gripping the handle of her leather briefcase, she squeezed her eyes shut again. The plane bumped, skidded, and the wheels screeched across the tarmac. There was a rush of noise as the plane taxied to a stop. Then everything was still.

She waited until she was absolutely positive that the plane had stopped moving and that she wasn't about to perish in a fiery crash.

Opening her eyes slowly, she stole a self-conscious glance at the pilot. Had he noticed that she was terrified out of her wits for no apparent reason?

The seat next to her was empty. She blinked, realizing the pilot had already gotten out of the plane.

How long had she been sitting here with her eyes tightly shut? She'd thought it had only been a few seconds, but maybe it had been longer.

Great.

She turned her head when the passenger-side plane door was opened from the outside. The pilot removed his sunglasses, and for the first time Melissa saw his eyes. They were aquamarine—a surprising light blue-green color, clear yet unfathomable at the same time.

Her heart beat hard against the wall of her chest with some sort of weird rush of . . . something edgy . . . and she forgot to be embarrassed about her behavior because she had no idea what was wrong with her now.

Was she sick?

Well, flying always made her feel weird and edgy and completely terrified. And she'd skipped lunch in her rush to get to the airfield in time.

That was all that was wrong with her. Had to be. What else could it be?

The man extended his hand to help her out, and uttered the first complete sentence she'd heard come out of his mouth since they'd met.

"Welcome," he drawled in a husky, seductive voice that made her think about whiskey and sex and old Southern plantations, "to Half Moon Island."

She took his hand. His grip was strong, warm, callused. A man's grip. An unexpected tingle sped up her arm.

How long had it been since she'd been touched by a handsome man—even if he was a little enigmatic and forbidding?

She felt positively melted as she stepped out of the

plane. Or maybe it was nothing more than the intense August sun she'd just stepped into.

It *was* hot. She could feel sweat beading on her brow, prickling between her breasts. The lightweight pastel suit she'd worn for today's meeting plastered stickily to her body. But the weather couldn't explain the strange feeling she had now as the pilot's strong hand gripped hers. It was as if there was some kind of electric current zipping between them.

But she didn't even know this man, she reminded herself, and she wasn't even sure she liked what she did know of him.

And he didn't seem to like her, either. There was some judgment in his eyes that she couldn't quite grasp. Disapproval almost, though that didn't make sense to her. He didn't know her any more than she knew him.

But she'd made a judgment about him, hadn't she?

It didn't matter, and she told herself to shake it off. So she'd rubbed this guy wrong, and he'd rubbed her wrong.

It wasn't important. "Thanks," she said briefly, pulling her hand away and glancing around. Okay, where was the house? Where was Leander Cox?

Apparently the toy tycoon hadn't come down to the airstrip to greet her. The airstrip itself appeared to exist in the middle of nowhere.

She looked around, seeing nothing but jungle to one side and beach to the other. And sparkling blue water beyond.

"Which way to the house?" she asked, pivoting back to the pilot. Apparently she was going to need his help whether she wanted it or not.

He folded his arms across his chest and leaned his shoulder casually against the wing of the plane. His stretchy white polo shirt, with the Cox Toys logo emblazoned on it, and denim shorts made it impossible not to notice his powerhouse body.

But Melissa was determined to achieve the impossible.

She glanced at the slim silver watch on her wrist.

"I have a meeting with Mr. Cox at three o'clock," she said pointedly. It was two forty-nine.

"I wouldn't worry about that meeting if I were you, Miss Parker."

Melissa lifted her gaze. The pilot remained in place, leaning against the plane, shadowed from the harsh sun. He looked relaxed and sexy, as if he belonged on a billboard wearing nothing but his briefs. Melissa felt like she was baking, and she was running out of patience with the way he was just standing there, staring at her with his ice-aqua eyes.

He was taller than she'd remembered from their brief meeting at the airfield. Or maybe he just seemed taller here on this tropical island where everything seemed wild and larger-than-life.

"Well, thank you, but I'll just go right ahead and worry." Melissa fought the apprehension building inside her.

What was this guy's problem? She needed to take control of this situation.

"I like to be punctual," she went on, "and it's nearly three now. Mr. Cox will be waiting for me. So if you don't mind—"

"Leander Cox isn't waiting for you," he told her casually. "He's not on the island. And there's no meeting. Never was."

Melissa gaped.

Leander Cox *had* to be on the island. There *had* to be a meeting. She'd gone to far too much trouble over this meeting already for him to be a no-show.

And why would the pilot even have taken her here if Leander Cox wasn't around and if there was no meeting?

No, this didn't make sense.

"What are you talking about?"

"I'm talking about Cooper Landon's wedding," the pilot said, straightening to advance toward her.

Her heart leaped into her throat and her mind spun.

"Cooper Landon's wedding," she repeated dizzily. "What about it?"

The pilot closed the distance between them with two long strides. His unfathomable gaze bored into her, and his nearness overwhelmed her. Her mouth went dry.

"You're not going to ruin it, that's what," he rasped quietly. "No more notes. No more phone calls. No more tantrums in front of the bride. And definitely no uninvited appearance at the church.''

Melissa stared at him, in shock from everything he'd just said. Her mind worked desperately to put it all together.

The whole thing had been a set-up.

Chapter Two

Melissa's pulse raced, but she did her best to act cool. As cool as the man in front of her, who now was talking like he could grind glass with his teeth. Gone was the seductive Southern drawl.

She didn't know if he was just putting her on, trying to scare her, or if he really was this tough. Either way, she *was* scared, so she supposed the answer didn't matter much.

Inhaling deeply, she forced herself to speak with a control she didn't feel.

"You're making a mistake," she said, noting that her voice was calm if a bit faint. "A really big one."

There was a crackle of light in his eyes that made her think he didn't give a flip what she thought.

"I'm not Dagmar," she went on even more calmly as she tried desperately to think of a way to prove that.

She didn't have her purse, or her identification. She didn't have so much as a library card. All she had was a briefcase full of designs and swatches and photographs. As usual, Dagmar's car had been in the shop awaiting repairs, and she'd begged to borrow Melissa's. Melissa had taken a taxi to the airfield— bringing only her briefcase with nothing more than cabfare and a lipstick.

And her wits. She had her wits. Surely she could make this man understand that he'd made a mistake.

But a hot wave of hysteria nearly overwhelmed her at the probing, disbelieving way he observed her, matching the disdain in his voice when he spoke.

"Cooper told me about your tricks, Dagmar, so don't bother. We're staying here, on Half Moon, till Cooper and his bride are safely away on their honeymoon."

"But I'm not Dagmar," she repeated.

He was planning to keep her here until after the wedding. Her, and this gorgeous maniac. Alone. All weekend.

The island had seemed dreamy and romantic in her mind, but in reality, it was like a nightmare. Primitive. And isolated.

She managed to go on speaking, though she had

no idea how. "This is a crime, you know. A serious crime. You can't keep me here all weekend against my will."

"Don't worry," he replied. "I'm not going to hurt you. Think of this as a vacation. It's a beautiful island." He swept an arm out toward the beach. "Sun, sand. People pay for this stuff."

Oh, yeah, she could just relax now.

"But this *isn't* a vacation." Not the one she'd been imagining, anyway. Melissa's thoughts raced as fast as her pulse. "It's kidnapping." The scary craziness of the situation frustrated her . . . and made her furious. "Aren't you worried about what's going to happen when we get back to Charleston? You could do a lot of time for kidnapping. Years."

He countered her smoothly. "This isn't kidnapping. This is engine trouble."

Melissa glared at him. "There's nothing wrong with that plane!" she informed him, irritated enough that she forgot to be afraid of him. "There's something wrong with your head. You're out of your mind. Take me back to Charleston. Now."

His brows spiked up his tanned forehead. "You want a crazy guy to fly you back to Charleston?"

A frustrated whoosh of breath exploded from her. "Okay," she managed desperately through tight lips, "I'll forget that you're insane if you'll forget that you're having 'engine trouble.' We'll both forget this whole thing. Deal?"

Brade tipped his head as if he were considering.

"No," he said finally. "That engine just doesn't sound right to me. I'll have to check it out. It'll probably take me 'til, oh, Sunday morning—when Cooper and his new bride will be leaving their wedding night suite to head off on their honeymoon. I suspect that right about the time they'll be leaving town, my plane should be back in working order. I'll take you back then."

"If there were really something wrong with your engine, you'd radio for help," she pointed out. "Everyone will know you're lying. You're going to jail. Down the river. For a very long time. I'll see to it."

His water-blue eyes narrowed to tiny glinting diamonds, and she remembered to be afraid of him again. His deadly calm demeanor made it clear that she wasn't in a good position to make threats.

"Now that would be your word against mine, wouldn't it?" he reminded her in a deceptively mild voice. "And since my radio isn't working"—he pulled a wire out of his pocket—"and since your reputation for wild antics precedes you, Dagmar, I'm not too concerned."

She swallowed thickly. His radio wasn't working. Oh, sure. Just like the engine. She had no idea how to operate a radio, anyway, but she'd been planning on making the attempt. But apparently he'd disabled the radio.

Unless she could get hold of that wire. She watched him put it back in his pocket.

As if I know how to enable the radio again, she thought hopelessly. As if she could even get the wire away from him in the first place.

But she couldn't accept defeat.

"I'm not Dagmar," she returned. Her voice was steady, thank goodness, but her heart was bouncing off her chest.

He didn't believe her. She had no idea how to make him believe her. The terrible truth was, she'd *told* him she was Dagmar at the outset.

The pilot—Brace or whoever he really was—put his sunglasses back on, but she could feel his piercing, watchful gaze just as if the lenses were nonexistent.

"Interesting," he said. "You look just like your picture."

Reaching into his other back pocket now, he pulled out his wallet and withdrew a small photo.

It was Dagmar, she realized when he held it out to her. Dagmar in a swimsuit. A bikini. Melissa recognized the picture. Dagmar had had her take it for Cooper.

With the sun behind Dagmar in the photo, shading her face while setting off her body to perfection, Melissa realized the image could just as easily be her. They both had shoulder-length blond hair and well-developed body types. As kids growing up together, they'd sometimes actually been mistaken as twins because they were the same age and had similar features.

She swallowed over the lump in her throat and

stared up at the hard face of the man in front of her. He was looking down at her as if she were a repeat offender in a courtroom denying the latest criminal charge.

"That's not me," she said, scared when she sounded unbelievable even to herself. She couldn't give up! "Okay, look, say that I *am* Dagmar," she said, going for a new approach, "let's just agree I've been scared straight. I'll never bother Cooper again. Okay? Let's go back to Charleston."

"Okay. Will do."

Relief swamped her and her jellied knees nearly gave out. Thank God he was seeing sense. She'd known, just known deep inside, that nothing this crazy could be happening to her.

Melissa Reynolds and this kind of trouble didn't meet. Not in this lifetime.

"On Sunday," he added.

Melissa's heart dropped to her feet. "Fine," she managed, mustering her wits. "Then I'm going back without you."

He lifted a sardonic brow.

"Really?"

"Really. What makes you think I can't fly that plane? For all you know, I could be a wonderful pilot. A phenomenal pilot. I could be doing aerobatics at airshows every weekend for all you know."

Even voicing the words made nausea well up in her throat.

"You're afraid of flying, aren't you?"

She hated him, she decided.

It was that simple.

"I'm *not* scared of flying," she lied through her teeth. "I'm going to get in that plane and take it back to Charleston."

He watched her, his pose completely relaxed.

"Okay."

Okay?

She wanted to cry—or hit him. Both, actually.

Unfortunately, she couldn't do either. Especially cry. She never cried—not in front of people, anyway.

"Fine." She strode around the plane and got in on the pilot's side, sliding smoothly onto the seat.

Her heart lunged up to her throat. She stared at the control panel. She had no idea what she was doing, but she was going to do something.

Something that would shake him up enough to make him get in the pilot's seat and take her straight back to Charleston.

She wished she'd paid more attention on the flight out. Did planes have keys, like cars? She didn't think so, but she didn't have the slightest idea.

Wildly, she punched some buttons. Nothing happened. He'd probably disabled the entire plane. Either that, or she was too technically challenged to even accidentally start a plane.

A scream ripped from her when the engine actually made a coughing sound.

She jerked back from whatever stray thing she'd touched that had caused the noise and pushed open the plane door, ejecting herself onto the tarmac—stumbling straight into his arms.

He staggered a bit as her full weight hit him, but he managed to keep them both upright. As his arms came around her, she pushed against his muscular chest. She felt the heat of his skin through his clothes, and the hardness of his body.

This close, she could see the imperfections of his stunning face—the small scar on his chin, the slight crookedness of his nose; and she could see his eyes through the dark lenses—and they held her.

Time froze for a wild second, then she pushed away from him, shocked. That same electricity zipped everywhere, making her feel weirdly dizzy, discombobulated, and angry. Really angry.

"Okay. You got me. I can't fly a plane." She smoothed her suit jacket with shaky fingers and tipped her chin, steadying her nerves. She'd had enough of this game for now. "Let's just go to the house."

There had to be a phone at the house, and Melissa intended to use it. She'd be out of here in no time.

"What house?" he inquired.

"Leander Cox's house!"

"Oh, you thought there was actually a house on Half Moon Island?"

Melissa gritted her teeth.

"Of course I thought there was a house!"

He'd *told* her there was a house. She didn't have

any doubt in her mind that he was the one who'd called, set up the appointment. Set up Dagmar.

"Don't worry," he said. "We're camping out. On the beach. It'll be fun."

Melissa wasn't a nature girl. She didn't do the outdoors. It was messy and unpredictable.

She liked everything neat and clean and oh-so-carefully-planned. Camping was not her idea of fun.

"You're not s-s-serious?" Now she really hated him. He had her so rattled, she was stammering.

Her childhood speech impediment had taken her most of a lifetime to overcome, and it had only taken minutes for this kidnapping creep to take all that hard work away from her. She couldn't remember the last time she'd relapsed.

She took a deep breath and said the next words slowly, deliberately, enunciating each word as if her life depended on it. And maybe it did.

"I'm not sharing a tent with you," she declared, sounding childish and more scared than she liked but at least she didn't stutter.

"We'll each have our own tent, of course," he informed her.

Something husky breathed into his voice, something that sounded like concern, and it surprised her. But when she looked into his face, she couldn't see any matching emotion there at all.

Whatever he'd felt—if he'd felt anything—he'd wiped it out as if it had never existed.

He still stood too close for comfort, still wore those

sunglasses that seemed to act as X-ray goggles, revealing all her weaknesses to her enemy.

"I told you, I'm not going to hurt you," he went on. "I'm not even going to touch you."

The griddle-hot day beat down on her. *I'm not even going to touch you.*

More sweat trickled between her breasts.

The heat was getting to her. It shimmered off the oily tarmac in waves around them.

"I don't know how to camp," she argued. "This isn't going to work, you know. What will we eat, drink? You're crazy!"

He shrugged. "There are streams with fresh water here. And there's plenty of fish in the ocean."

Streams and fish?

That was it. Melissa had to get out of here. She couldn't do this. The whole situation gave her the heebie-jeebies.

"If you're so convinced that Dagmar is going to do something to ruin Cooper's wedding," she said, trying a new tack, "aren't you just a teeny bit concerned about what's going to happen if you have the wrong woman?"

He blew off her suggestion.

"Nice try, Dagmar."

"I'm n-not—" She stopped short and slowed down. "I'm *not* Dagmar."

He looked her over, and she steeled herself against his gaze. She was used to men looking at her. She didn't think she was vain, but she knew men found

her attractive. Enough of them came on to her for
her to understand that much. But she didn't feel that
same kind of heated interest now. There was a certain
coldness in his observation, as if he had no use for
her.

She must have imagined the concern on his face
a few minutes before. This guy wasn't even human.

"So," he drawled, "you just go around introducing
yourself to people at airfields as Dagmar, and attending meetings as Dagmar. And to top it off, you
just happen to look like Dagmar."

"You don't understand," she said desperately. "Let
me explain. Dagmar wanted to see Cooper one more
time, and I thought if she did, she would finally face
facts, give up on him. And you—it was you who called,
wasn't it?"

His hard face registered no acknowledgement of
her charge.

"You were so insistent that Mr. Cox had to have
Dagmar . . ." she went on. "Don't you see? It's a mess
on the surface, but it's really quite simple once you
understand. I'm not Dagmar. You've made a terrible
mistake. Take me back to Charleston, and we'll
straighten it out."

He turned, half-climbed into the plane and pulled
something out of the back.

"You're very convincing, Dagmar," he com-
mented.

"Stop calling me Dagmar. My name is Melissa.
Melissa Reynolds. I'm Dagmar's cousin and partner.

I took her place today. Can't you just—plug back in
that radio wire or whatever you have to do to make
it work—and call somebody? Call Cooper?"

"It's a radio, not a phone," he answered curtly.

He shoved the duffel into her arms. She took it
automatically.

Not that he gave her much choice.

"What's this?" she asked.

"Clothes. Your tent. A few necessities. I told you,
it's going to be just like a vacation. Consider me your
travel agent. I even packed for you."

"You're such a thoughtful kidnapper," she bit out,
all too aware that her honest explanation was having
no effect. Although she was relieved that she wasn't
going to have to spend the next forty-eight hours in
this suit. No way was she going to thank him for
anything, though.

And she certainly wasn't going to give up on getting
out of here. She wasn't about to spend the entire
weekend with Mr. Personality.

For one thing, she was supposed to meet Dagmar
back at the office this afternoon. When she didn't
show up, Dagmar would worry.

Dagmar would send help ... *if Dagmar didn't get
sidetracked and forget about her.* That prospect worried
her. Her cousin wasn't famous for being responsible.

Especially lately, when she was so obsessed with
Cooper Landon.

But there was still the radio. If help didn't come
by tonight, he'd go to sleep eventually, wouldn't he?

She'd get that wire away from him, and she'd figure out how to use it—if it killed her.

Or him.

Preferably him.

She'd drop the topic of the radio for now, lull him into thinking she'd forgotten about it. But she was leaving this island—and she was determined to do it before Sunday.

Melissa felt better instantly. She had a plan.

She was getting help, getting out of here, and she was going to send Brade's sexy, sarcastic, way-too-fine self to the pokey.

"I'll mention your kindness to the parole board," she added super-sweetly.

He shut the plane hatch and shot her a darkly amused glance.

"Coop didn't tell me you were funny," he said.

And he took off toward the beach.

Chapter Three

She was going to drive him crazy.

Brade strolled up the sun-drenched beach and had to wonder if the next forty-eight hours were going to be more than he'd bargained for. He hadn't expected to like Dagmar Parker. And he didn't, thank God.

She was obviously a self-absorbed brat, and there was no way he'd ever like her.

But something was eating at him, had been ever since she'd walked up to his plane at Fortin Airfield and smiled at him.

Her smile.

Everything else about Dagmar Parker was as he'd

expected—her honey gold hair, her sensuous body, even her exotic velvet-dark eyes.

But that smile had belied it all. That soft, shaky smile had whispered of vulnerability and a depth of feeling he didn't want to know about.

That smile had touched him, and made him angry. But *nothing* touched him. He didn't let anything touch him, hadn't in the last five years.

He reminded himself that Dagmar Parker's vulnerable smile was probably as superficial as the rest of her. She might be most men's idea of a walking dream, but she wasn't his, and luckily she wasn't Coop's, at least not anymore.

It was Brade's job to keep her from ruining the new happiness his best friend had found. He couldn't let feelings—especially feelings he neither wanted nor trusted—get in the way.

He'd made a point of speaking to her as little as possible on the flight over, but avoiding her now that they were actually on the island was going to be a lot more difficult. He was definitely going to avoid touching her again.

What in the world had that unmistakable electricity been all about?

When he'd helped her out of the plane, then again when she fallen straight into his chest, he'd felt like he'd been zapped by mini-bolts of lightning.

Maybe he was just more exhausted from overwork than he'd realized.

"Excuse me!" she called.

He kept walking.

"Brade!" She ran up beside him, carrying her strappy sandals in one hand, the duffel clutched in the other. He'd shucked his own shoes along the way, too. "Excuse me, Mr. Kidnapper!" she called, catching up to him. "Just where are we going?"

The sun glinting off her golden hair made her look deceptively angelic. Just like that smile of hers.

"There's a cove up here," he said, staring straight ahead again, not giving himself a chance to be pulled back into the uncomfortable emotions she evoked. "Good fishing, rocks to shelter our tents against. Nearby freshwater stream."

"I see." She kept pace with him, her lithe legs keeping up easily now that she'd removed her shoes. "So you've been here before? Camping?"

Brade made a noncommittal grunt. He didn't want to chat. He didn't want to get to know Dagmar Parker, or let her get to know him. Personal conversation was strictly off-limits.

"Oh, yes, Melissa," she answered for him, stressing her name and hoping he would get the point. "I come here all the time. I bring all my abductees here."

He shot her a look.

"That's right," he said agreeably. He didn't like it that he wanted to laugh. He wasn't going to pretend camaraderie with her. "All of them. I'll show you where I bury them later."

That shut her up.

They reached the cove, which wasn't much more than a sandy inlet. The water was shallow and clear, making spearfishing easy. The nearby jungle provided a source of wood for fires, and the beach rose up to gigantic boulders shaded by overhanging palms. A perfect shelter from the wind. Further in, a waterfall gushed from between the rocks, providing easy access to drinkable water.

It was a private place where he'd spent a lot of time in the past, and Brade didn't realize he was going to resent bringing this stranger here until that very moment.

He felt invaded.

"We're here," he said gruffly. He set his duffel down and examined the site, determining the exact location where he'd make camp. "Set up your tent."

"I don't know how."

He turned. She'd stopped several feet behind him, her strappy sandals still dangling from one hand, the duffel dropped at her feet now. That vague vulnerabilty of hers shadowed the brown depths of her eyes, but her spine was stiff and proud.

And for a moment, he found himself respecting her.

"So watch me," he said, and turned back around, irritated. He pulled the small pouch containing the one-man tent out of his duffel.

"Okay, but . . ."

There was a long silence and he had to look at her again.

"Well, I have another problem first," she said finally, all in a rush.

Her face heated visibly.

"What?" he asked, his voice surly and he noticed the tightness in her throat as she swallowed in response to his tone. He intimidated her without even trying.

That didn't make him feel good, but he wasn't going to do anything to change it.

She lifted her chin and her cheeks turned an even brighter pink.

"I need to go to the bathroom."

"So go," he said, and nodded his head toward the jungle.

Her delicate brows rose instantly.

"I can't go in there!" she cried, looking horrified and disgusted. "I mean, didn't you bring some, I don't know, some special bathroom tent or something?"

Brade felt laughter burning at the back of his throat. "Sure," he said when he had it under control. "It's between the spa tent and the movie theatre tent."

She stared at him as if he was speaking a foreign language.

"You've got to be kidding!"

"Okay, you've got me," he deadpanned. "There's no spa tent, no movie tent. I was kidding."

A markedly unfeminine sound of frustration erupted from his captive, who proceeded to flounce off in the direction of the palm trees.

"Hey!" Brade picked up her duffel, pulled out the tent, then closed it back up and tossed it after her. She turned around, murder written on her face.

She looked petulant and rebellious and completely beautiful. A tightness crept up his thighs.

"You might as well get changed while you're at it," he told her curtly, and went back to his work.

She was going to kill him.

Melissa didn't know how she was going to do it yet, but she had ideas and she was going to work on them.

He deserved to die. No, he deserved to suffer, she corrected herself—just as he was making her suffer. He had no consideration.

No courtesy. No human kindness.

And apparently, no conscience.

She stripped off her suit jacket behind one of the huge boulders. There was no way she was going into that jungle to change clothes. The jungle was dark and tangled and creepy-looking.

Water gurgled from a nearby stream that spilled over the rocks and down into the cove in a waterfall that she might have found enchanting in another lifetime. The jungle awaited on one side while the beach dropped off to the other.

She was stuck out here, in plain sight, with nothing more than a big rock to provide privacy. She peered over her shoulder nervously.

If he dared come spy on her, she *would* kill him. With her bare hands if she had to.

Leaning a little farther, she could see him down at the cove. He almost had his tent set up already. Great. He'd done it while she wasn't watching. He'd told her to watch, but then he'd sent her off to change clothes.

Probably his concept of a joke.

This whole thing seemed to be some big game to him. She could hardly miss the mockery in his voice, the contempt in his eyes, whenever he spoke to her.

Fuming, she ducked back to check out the contents of the duffel. There were Cox Toys T-shirts and a couple pairs of denim shorts in a size that was close enough to her own.

There was white cotton underwear, a pair of watershoes that were a size too small for her, and a bag that contained basic toiletries.

Making use of the supplies made her feel a little as if she was giving in to this insanity, validating it somehow. But under the circumstances, she knew it would be even more insane to spend another minute wearing her suit. She wasn't exactly attending a business meeting anymore.

She was attending . . . a weekend from hell.

Stepping out of her skirt, she dropped it by the duffel. She couldn't believe this was happening. Her mind simply couldn't comprehend it. She felt as if her life had gotten on the wrong bus, and it was speeding out of control.

A barely perceptible rustle from the underbrush near the trees had her spinning back around. A small lizard slithered through the bushy weeds.

Its beady, irridescent eyeballs locked on her, its tail twitching like a little whip, then the grotesque creature scuttled off.

Melissa froze, her hand paralyzed in the process of undoing the top button of her now-sticky blouse, staring after the disgusting little reptile.

Something tickled her toe and she all but leaped out of her skin. She definitely ascended a good foot in the air, landing with a whomp on her butt when she came back down.

The source of her trouble, some sort of hairy millipede, wiggled away. She got up, rubbing her sore bottom.

She hated reptiles! And bugs! And tents!

And men.

One man, anyway.

This was all Brade's fault, and he would pay. She'd make sure of it.

Back on her feet, she finished unbuttoning her blouse and flung it after the skirt. She was down to her bra and panties, in the middle of nowhere.

There was a distant buzz overhead, and it took only seconds for her to recognize the miraculous sound of potential rescue.

She didn't think twice. Or once, for that matter.

"A plane!" she whispered, then she was shrieking . . . and running.

Chapter Four

Brade watched as Dagmar burst out from behind a boulder and all but flung herself down the embankment toward the beach, waving and yelling. His only thought was that she was crazy, until he realized she was chasing after the airplane.

When she reached level ground, she started jumping up and down. Brade set down the tools he'd been using to construct his tent, straightened, and couldn't help but stare.

Her attempt to get help would be fruitless. The jet was probably flying at least six or seven thousand feet above them—close enough for them to hear the engine noise but too far for anyone to really see her.

What was holding Brade's attention wasn't her laughable effort. It was the fact that she was making it in nothing but her bra and panties. Nothing but her lace, delectably barely-there bra and panties.

He broke out in a sweat and his chest tightened. Dagmar Parker was a kook, just like her reputation. So why couldn't he seem to keep his eyes off her? Disliking her should have made him immune, but his physical response made it clear he wasn't.

It was natural, he supposed, looking for a rational explanation. He was a man in the prime of his life. And it had been so long since he'd been with a woman. Not since Rebecca. Not once.

What else could explain his body's reaction other than deprivation? He preferred to be a machine, going through the motions every day since his life, effectively, had ended five years ago at the same time Rebecca's had.

But this weird woman was reminding him that he was a man, with all the natural needs of any man.

It certainly could not mean that he wanted *her*. She was the wrong woman in the wrong place at the wrong time when his body had just happened to decide to wake up.

He'd deal with it the way he dealt with everything, by exerting self-control. The fact that she hated him would definitely be a plus.

The plane disappeared into the distance, and Dagmar's agitated leaps in the air got lower and lower until she stopped waving and jumping at all. Her slender shoulders slumped for a moment, and Brade was shocked to find himself filled with an empty, restless, inexplicable yearning to hold her, comfort her in her disappointment. Which was patently ridiculous since her disappointment was over her inability to escape him.

Her spine straightened and she turned. Her fiery-dark eyes locked on him and she charged across the beach toward him with her beautiful bare body and her pursed, pink lips—like a cross between a primitive goddess and an angry schoolmarm.

And how that combination could be so sensual, Brade had no idea. But his palms were sweating and his stomach muscles were contracting and his self-control was being utilized to the max . . . because he was not, absolutely not, going to let himself look at those full breasts bursting out of that lacy, frothy brassiere.

So he looked at her face as she stopped in front of him, her cheeks flushing hotly, and for a second the roar of the pounding surf seemed to be coming from inside his head.

"That was probably a search plane," she clipped out fiercely when she reached him, pointing toward the vanishing contrail. "They're looking for me already. You should take me back now, before it's too late."

He shrugged and spoke in an indifferent tone that was far from the reality of his inner turmoil.

"For your information," he drawled, "that was a passenger jet."

She jutted her jaw at him.

"Whatever. Someone *will* be searching for me. Soon."

"You could be right," he replied, angry at himself because he was having such a hard time focusing on this conversation. The problem was, he decided, that she needed clothes. Her near-nakedness was playing havoc with his senses and his willpower. "But I doubt it," he continued tensely. "In the meantime, if you know what's good for you, you'll get dressed—and *stay* dressed."

Melissa's heart practically stopped.

An endless beat passed wherein she realized that she was standing in front of this man, this barbarian, in nothing but her underwear!

How could she have done this?

She'd been so excited about the plane—

She couldn't help herself. She had to look to see his expression. His ice-aqua eyes flared with some kind of dangerous energy she couldn't read, but could feel nonetheless—down to every last quivering nerve end in her body.

But they weren't even touching this time!

She looked down, to avoid his gaze as well as to make a panicky check of herself. All the important parts were covered, but it was still embarrassing, particularly since she was a rather modest person to begin with.

Folding her arms over her chest, she made a last-ditch attempt to maintain some decency. She went for a diversionary tactic.

"If I know what's good for me?" Melissa repeated, determined not to be intimidated by the fact that she was standing there in her underwear—a point which she was not going to openly acknowledge. If there was one thing she was hanging on to, it was her dignity. "Oh please. I'm not afraid of you."

She started to stomp by, but Brade grabbed her arm, catching her in a grip of steel. All her thoughts scattered as he locked his gaze on her and didn't let go. She was taller than average, but he still towered over her.

Something shadowed those aqua eyes, taking all the spark and glimmer away—and the electricity with it. But she felt drawn anyway—drawn to something that was actually . . . painful. This, she sensed sharply, was the real Brade. The man behind the action hero body and the arresting eyes.

Or was she nuts?

The idea of Brade being a man who felt pain, and thus joy and every other emotion that she felt, made him too human. She didn't want him to be human. It would make everything too complicated.

She wanted to keep her emotions simple, but she had an instinctive feeling that Brade wasn't a simple man. There was depth to his darkness and she found herself more curious about him than she wanted to be.

"Maybe you should be afraid of me," he went on to advise curtly.

"I don't scare easily," she returned, yanking her arm free of his unwelcome grip. "Maybe it's you who's scared of me."

"Keep your clothes on, Dagmar. And neither one of us will have anything to be scared of."

She lifted her chin, telling herself he couldn't possibly know that her legs felt like limp spaghetti, that she was indeed scared of him—on more than one level. That even the thick, creepy jungle was starting to look good in comparison.

He couldn't know any of it, and he wouldn't, not if she kept her head on straight.

"Melissa," she said, mustering her courage and her spine. "Call me *Melissa.*"

And she tromped off across the sand in her bra and panties as if she were exiting a boardroom in a suit.

She came back carrying a rock.

Brade watched Dagmar-or-Melissa-or-whatever-she-called-herself-at-the-moment emerge—fully clothed, thank the island gods—hoisting the biggest rock she was probably capable of budging.

The small but firm muscles in her arms tightened under the load, and he could see her sweating. He could also hear her murmuring numerous unladylike things under her breath, mostly about him, but she kept going without deigning to so much as glance his way. Curiously, he watched her place the rock on the beach and go back.

She repeated the process and after a few times he realized she was spelling out the word *help*.

He couldn't restrain a momentary impulse to admire her for her determination. She was nothing if not resourceful, and she had a lot more guts and strength of will than he'd expected. He'd expected hysterics and tantrums out of her, not physical labor.

But Brade was not going to start liking her, so admiring her was out of the question.

He pushed away the stupid impulse to do just that. Spelling out H-E-L-P in rocks on the sand was just another loony strategy and he shouldn't be surprised by anything Coop's ex-girlfriend came up with.

The effort wouldn't do her any good, of course. For one thing, the rocks were almost the same color as the sand. The few planes that passed over the island would never be able to read her plea.

Besides, her message would be too low on the shore. The tide would wash it out tonight.

But the job kept her busy, and kept her out of his hair. That was a good thing.

He was about to head toward the trees, determined to gather some firewood, when she dropped a rock.

On her foot.

There was no doubt in his mind that she was in

pain when he ran to where she'd slid, gasping, to the sand. Her eyes were shiny with tears she held back.

"Are you okay?"

She was barefoot, and he knelt, ran his fingers lightly over the reddened, already bruising injury from the dropped rock. From his position leaning toward her, his head was close, too close, to hers. She smelled sweet and fruity, and her skin felt like satin.

Her small foot was perfectly formed and for a second, as he held it, he imagined massaging it. . . .

The electrical sensations hit him like a rain of bullets and he nearly recoiled from the sheer sensation of physical assault.

He shook himself.

"Can you move your toes?"

She swallowed and glanced down at her foot. He followed her gaze, watched her neat, peach-polished toes wriggle while he supported her injured foot. And despite the fact that there was nothing obviously sensual about the situation, a treacherous craving inside him grew worse the longer he was in contact with her.

"I don't think it's broken." He released his hold as quickly as he could without causing her any additional pain.

The desire inside him subsided, and so did the electrical zippiness.

Distance. It was all he needed. No looking, no touching.

"I don't think so either," she said, looking at him

oddly. Then the familiar attitude was back in her voice. "Of course, if you want to have it looked at by a doctor just to be sure, we'd better head for the plane."

"Good one," he conceded, brushing the sand off himself and rising. "But I don't think so."

"I'll keep trying," she promised softly.

He knew she would. And that was exactly what he was afraid of.

Chapter Five

Melissa set the last rock in place and collapsed back on the beach to survey her handiwork.

From the corner of her eye, she sneaked a look at Brade. He'd finished building a firepit and was doing something with a long stake.

It looked as if he was sharpening it. For what purpose, she couldn't imagine.

The last time she'd seen a stake like that, she'd been watching a vampire movie marathon on late-night cable.

She didn't figure Brade was planning to go vampire hunting, so that stake had to be for something else. She had a bad feeling it had something to do with the fish he'd mentioned, but didn't want to dwell on it. The whole idea of dinner anyone had just caught made her queasy. Whatever Brade had in mind, she wasn't sure she was up to it. She was a packaged food kind of girl.

What she wouldn't give for some peanut butter and crackers now.

She looked back at her appeal in the sand, focusing on her main problem—getting the heck out of here. Perhaps her efforts had been wasted at best, she knew, and hopeless at worst. But it had been the only thing she could think of.

Her entire body ached as a result of what was probably a futile exercise.

Sitting there, rubbing her neck in an attempt to ease her tight shoulder muscles and keep her mind off Brade's dinner plans, she realized there was actually a gorgeous sunset right in front of her.

A palette of incredible color rippled over the ocean. They were on the the eastern side of Half Moon, but still the sun dipping below the western horizon created shimmers of gold in the shadows of the deepest indigo blues she'd ever seen.

Quite simply, it took her breath away.

The blues and blacks only made the shimmery flecks that slipped over the horizon that much more beautiful. The panorama of the vast ocean gave her a sense of boundless space that was both startling and eerie. For a moment, she allowed herself to be transported by the view, to simply stare and appreciate.

Her stomach growled, taking her out of her reverie. The radiance of the scene disappeared as the reality of her situation returned full force.

Melissa thought about the radio wire. It was one thing to decide she'd get it back from the man. It was another thing to accomplish the task. She'd have to wait until the middle of the night to try to steal it away from him in his sleep. She'd have to actually crawl in, and take it right off his body.

What if he woke up, caught her?

But it was her only hope. She had to take the risk.

She perched on one of the small boulders near the firepit and wondered if Dagmar had missed her yet. If Dagmar had even remembered to come back to the office to meet her and return the car.

Brade was completely ignoring her and hadn't even looked up when she'd come strolling across the beach. She'd been thinking about what her uninhibited cousin would do in this situation, and she'd found herself almost instinctively swinging her hips. That was what Dagmar would do. She would swing her hips, bat her eyes, wrap Brade right around her little finger and have him flying her back to Charleston before he knew what had hit him.

But truthfully, Melissa wasn't comfortable employing her feminine wiles, such as they were. She was modest about her sexuality.

Actually, she was uptight, she thought to herself with a sigh. Really uptight.

Okay, she was a virgin.

She'd have to rely on her wits. What had she been thinking when she'd tried that hip-swinging thing, anyway? She was no femme fatale.

Besides, she had her doubts about whether Brade could be so easily persuaded.

He was sharpening another stick, and he'd lit the fire. Sparks flew in the dusky light and the flames crackled pleasantly. The corrugated muscles in his forearms were powerful by any standard, and strangely beautiful. She found herself too easily mesmerized by the repetitive movements of his work, watching the flex and pull of his powerful shoulders and arms.

She shook herself out of it.

"So when's dinner?" she asked without thinking, blurting out the first thing that came to her in order to distract herself from his impressive body. Besides, the silent treatment was making her nervous.

"Whenever you catch it," he said without looking up.

This didn't sound promising.

He straightened, handed her the stake he'd been sharpening. "This one's yours," he said.

She took it dubiously, mostly because he didn't give her much choice with the way he shoved it at her.

"You don't really expect me to, um . . . stab a fish with this?" Melissa recoiled from the idea.

She was a vegetarian, but not a strict one. She ate seafood pretty often when she went out to restaurants, so some people wouldn't even consider her a vegetarian at all.

But this wasn't a restaurant. This wasn't stuffed flounder from the menu.

This was gore-your-own.

"I don't think so," she said. "I'll just head back to the hotel, order off the room service menu."

"There's no room service here," he said curtly. "You want to eat, you get your own food."

Melissa swallowed. Was he serious?

"You've got some backup in your duffel, though, right? Some cookies? Chips?"

"Junk," he said. "That stuff'll kill you."

He was a health nut. Who'd have guessed?

She tried to think of something healthy.

"Granola bars?" She chewed her bottom lip and heard her stomach rumble.

If he heard it, he didn't show it.

"I've got some buckwheat mush for breakfast," he told her. "That's it."

Buckwheat mush?

"Great. That's my favorite."

If he picked up on the sarcasm, he didn't show it.

"Time to go fishing," he said briskly. "That is, if you're hungry."

Weakness washed over her. She *was* hungry.

She reminded herself that her goal was to get

through the evening. Then she'd steal the radio wire, call for help and send him to the slammer.

It would work.

It had to work.

He was already walking off. So much for preprandial chitchat. She had to admit it, she was starting to miss normal human conversation. She was a little insecure sometimes, but she really was a people person.

And from all appearances, Brade was not.

She watched him stalk down the shoreline. The fish in the cove, even in the dusky light, were easily visible in the clear, shallow water at the end of the inlet. He walked slowly, deliberately, seeming to study his prey.

She almost jumped out of her skin when, after only a few moments, he made an abrupt thrust at the water. He came up with a small but fat fish, which he promptly took back to the firepit.

That he displayed so many wilderness skills didn't surprise her at this point. She already knew that he was an intriguing combination of civilization and savagery, although he was connected with Cox Toys in some way, obviously.

He had access to the Cox Toys plane. She'd been guessing he was Leander Cox's private pilot. Obviously, he was a trained, educated man.

But Brade was also dark and incomprehensible and untamed, ready and able to live off the land—and use whatever means suited his ends. And he had the body to back him up.

What did surprise her was that he came back to her and offered to help.

"It's not as easy as it looks," he said, coming up from behind, using quick, precise movements to reconfigure her grip on the stake. His voice was still gruff, as if even when doing a kindness he couldn't soften. "You're holding the thing all wrong, anyway."

Melissa tried to focus on the fish in the water, but it was difficult over the frantic beat of her heart. His touch evoked strange and unaccountable electrical sensations within her, and she felt vibrantly, shockingly alive everywhere his flesh touched hers.

"This isn't your everyday skill," she replied, surprised at how breathy she sounded. "Who are you, Tarzan?"

"Not quite," he said, and she detected a smile in his voice which blurred that hard edge. "I'm a city boy, born and bred. Watch that one," he said, diverting them back to the subject at hand. "You have to be prepared to move fast when one comes in range."

She sensed he didn't want to have a personal conversation.

Too bad. She did. "Charleston?" she probed.

"Charleston," he agreed. "And Savannah."

"You moved around." She watched a fish swimming just out of her range, but she was thinking about the man behind her.

"No, it was just a matter of which parent I was

living with at the time," he answered. He stepped back, releasing her. "Get ready," he said.

"Your parents were divorced?" She turned around, forgetting about the fish, telling herself it was nothing more than simple human curiosity. "What about you?" she fired another question at him. "Are you married, divorced, single?"

"Drop the questions." He clearly wasn't pleased, and the edge in his voice was sharper than ever.

"Why?" she asked, surprised that she actually felt a little hurt by his tone.

"I don't like questions."

"Why?" She tilted her head to look up at Brade, and was shocked to see that shadowy lost look in the back of his eyes for just a second before he glowered at her yet again.

She hadn't been nuts. There really was something haunting the man.

Not that she cared. She was just curious, that's all. And he didn't have to be so rude.

"You'd better get your dinner," he said curtly. "Or you'll go hungry. It's going to be dark soon and you won't be able to see the fish."

He turned away, heading back to the firepit. She saw him withdraw a huge leather-sheathed knife from his duffel and begin to clean the fish he'd caught.

He couldn't see her, and she'd had enough. Behind his back, Melissa stuck her tongue out at him.

Unfortunately, it didn't make her feel one whit better.

* * *

Damn her.

Damn her for her irritating, relentless conversation and her fearless, breathtaking eyes and her soft, vulnerable beauty.

And Brade damned himself for not being able to ignore her, even when he pretended to do just that. He'd known every move she'd made, every breath she took.

She'd failed to catch a single thing despite her laughable efforts with the fishing spear. He'd never seen anyone more uncoordinated in his life. No wonder she'd dropped a rock on her foot! He was surprised she hadn't stabbed herself with the damn spear.

He shared his simple meal with her. He thought at first she wouldn't accept his offering, but hunger had obviously won out.

From that point, the meal had been conducted in silence, which baffled him after her earlier chattiness. If she was trying to confuse him, she was doing a fine job. He couldn't keep up with her moods.

Long after she'd set up her tent, jerry-rigging it with some extra sticks he'd brought for firewood rather than asking him for help to do it right, he sat moodily by the firepit listening to the ocean crash on the beach. The tide was coming in, and all he could think about was how it had felt to have his arms around her.

And even now he wasn't sure if he'd really been trying to teach her how to fish, or if he'd just been using the excuse to touch her.

Damn her.

It was going to be a long night.

Chapter Six

By touch Melissa found the tiny button on the side
of her watch, pressing it to illuminate the face. Two
A.M. It had taken all of her willpower to stay awake
this long.

Dragging rocks around to make that rescue message had exhausted her, and her body was screaming
for sleep. Her eyes felt gritty, her muscles ached, and
she felt sticky from the bug repellent she'd applied
liberally after a mosquito had found its way inside
her tent. Luckily, Brade seemed to have thought of
all the basics when he'd packed her toiletries.

Of course, Melissa's list of bare necessities normally
included Twinkies and TV. She was adjusting, albeit

temporarily. She'd even enjoyed the fish Brade had speared, which surprised her. After watching him lop off its head, she hadn't been sure she could actually eat it.

Hunger had won out. She didn't know if it was the freshness, or the outdoor grilling, but she couldn't remember tasting better—not even in Charleston's finest seafood restaurants.

Not that she'd said so to Brade. She'd been deliberately incommunicative. She'd had enough of his rebuffs.

It had been hours after dinner before he'd retired to his tent. He'd lingered by the fire until Melissa had begun to think he would never go to bed. His profile had been shadowed, remote, somehow sad.

Curiosity had hit her again, more sharply now as she'd watched him through the sliver-thin opening in her tent flaps. What did he think about as he gazed into the dying fire?

What kept him awake and alone late into the night?

But she didn't voice her questions. He'd made it abundantly clear that he wasn't interested in talking to her. In fact, he wasn't interested in her, period. He didn't like her, trust her, believe her.

And Melissa didn't care. Or at least, she didn't want to think she did.

So she'd waited.

Finally she'd watched him crawl into his tent, and she'd forced herself to wait over another hour after that, measuring time by the pounding of the surf.

She hoped he was asleep now, because if he wasn't, she was about to be. If she didn't act pretty soon, it would be too late.

Not a peep had come from his tent, so she had to assume he was asleep and act now—or give it up. And she wasn't going to give it up.

She just hoped he was a sound sleeper. If not, she'd be in trouble. She was sure he wouldn't welcome her waking him up.

The night air was warm, and her breath felt thick in her lungs despite the soft sea breeze. Her pulse raced again, adrenaline surging into her system as she slipped from her tent.

She was barefoot, still dressed in her T-shirt and shorts. He hadn't provided her any nightwear, and she wondered for a second what he had on.

Surely he was still wearing his clothes, too?

What if he slept in the nude?

Her heart jumped into her throat.

He couldn't possibly be naked, she reassured herself. And if he was, then getting the radio wire would be that much easier because his shorts wouldn't be on his body.

Melissa took a deep breath. And another, slowly exhaling each time until the blood pounding in her ears settled to a dull roar.

She crept toward Brade's tent, moonlight guiding her path across the sand. She gave a quick glance at the sky, remembering to be grateful for the natural night-light. It would also guide her trek back to the plane, since she had no flashlight.

Moonlight wasn't something she'd thought much about before. In the city, she never noticed it, camouflaged as it was by the burning blaze of streetlights.

She'd never seen so many stars before, either. The heavens were sprinkled liberally with bright, glowing beacons. For a second, she wished she'd paid more attention in her high school science classes. For the first time in her life, she could see the stars, really see them—and she'd love to be able to pick out the Big Dipper, or Orion's Belt, or . . . whatever those other things up there were called.

But she didn't have the slightest idea, or even time to try to figure it out. She had a mission—she was heading straight back for the neon city. Just as soon as she picked Brade's pocket.

She sneaked around the side of his tent. She knew someday she would laugh about this. She tried to imagine sitting around with Dagmar, drinking mocha lattes and talking about the night she'd escaped from Half Moon Island. Using the technique she'd employed often in the earliest stages of developing Carolina Chic—back when it was more dream than reality—she used visualization to imagine that she'd already achieved her goal. This weekend was in the past, over, done with. She was in her office at Carolina Chic, and Brade was in the hoosegow.

Her pulse slowed, and she took another deep

breath as she crouched toward the opening of his tent. Leaning her ear against the canvas, she listened.

At first, she could hear nothing, only the unending rhythm of the surf. Then, slowly, she picked out steady breaths, soft and even. She dared to peek between the canvas flaps, through the zipped mosquito mesh, into the darkness within the tent where she could just make out his form in the shadows. He lay on his side, facing away from her. She opened the flaps a little wider, and moonlight filtered in.

Fortunately, he was fully clothed, as he rested atop an air mattress identical to the one he'd provided for her. The night was warm, and like her, he'd decided against slipping inside the sleeping bag.

She unzipped the mosquito netting a fraction of an inch at a time, and stuck her head inside the tent.

His considerable frame seemed to fill the space. His tent was every bit the same size as hers, but it felt smaller, lots smaller, with both of them inside it.

Seeing him there, sleeping peacefully, gave her a strange feeling. There was something intimate about watching someone sleep. With his eyes shut and the hard line of his mouth relaxed, he actually looked . . . a little bit vulnerable.

Melissa told herself not to be silly.

But she remembered the dark, glittering, almost painful emotion she'd seen in his eyes, and she knew she was wrong.

All that moody concentration hid . . . *something*.

For a moment, she stared at him, taking in the

harsh planes and angles of his face, softer now in repose. This was the first time she'd had a chance to look, really look, at him without him looking back. It hit her again how gorgeous he was. His features were stark, but somehow mesmerizing. He was much too handsome.

As she watched, he shifted in his sleep, turning toward her. Her breath jammed in her throat, but he didn't open his eyes, settled back into the same regular breathing pattern.

Get to work, she warned herself. What was she doing, wasting time gawking at the man? He was gorgeous, but dangerous. She had no time to gawk, and no time to wonder about his private pain. Who cared about his pain, anyway?

She'd seen him put the radio wire in his back left pocket. Now, she just prayed it was still there.

And that she had the nerve to get it out.

Carefully, she crawled further inside, her feet sticking out of the tent opening. In the shadows, she was going to have to rely on touch.

Her pulse started banging again. She tried to flick a switch in her mind, back to visualization.

This was all over. She'd accomplished the mission. She'd found the radio wire and successfully reconnected it. Help was on the way.

But all she could visualize was touching Brade's backside. His very fine—in fact, awesome—backside. No, she wasn't projecting into the future at all. She was definitely living in the present.

She was, for all intents and purposes, about to cop a feel!

A bubble of something filled her throat, and she realized in dismay what it was. Giggles. This was no time for a set of nervous giggles!

She swallowed the ludicrous bubble down. This was business.

Trying not to make a noise, she took another deep breath and crawled a few inches closer. Slowly, she reached for his pocket, barely skimming her fingers across the material.

The wire was small, light, and she couldn't tell if it was still there through the denim.

Now that he was facing her, she had to reach around him. He was too close to the side of the tent for her to get what she wanted from the other direction. She was inches from him, and with the low height of the tent, she had to rest on one elbow, almost prone beside him, as she reached resolutely over his hips toward the rear pocket.

Her fingers slid inside the taut denim pocket, creeping downward. She felt the tip of the wire! It was still there! She wiggled her index finger, trying to loop it around a twist in the wire. Then she had it and began slowly, cautiously, to pull it out.

Success was a second away—

Brade's arm came out of nowhere, wrapping around her like a vise, and the next thing she knew she was flat on her back with his lean, mean body on top of her. A yelp jammed halfway up her throat.

He was awake!

Melissa was ready for him to be angry, ready for him to bellow and roar and throw her out of his tent on her rear.

What she wasn't ready for was his kiss.

Chapter Seven

The woman tasted like life—full of promise and hope and forgotten pleasures. She was a dream, and he knew that. But it didn't matter. Not now, not when she felt so real in his arms.

He could feel everything as if it were really happening—her plump breasts crushing against his chest, her pounding heartbeats, her soft breaths that he caught in his mouth as he plundered her sweet lips.

It had been so long . . . too long. He kissed her, hard and deep, need surging through his body. It was all he could do, all he could imagine doing.

With one hand still tangled gently in her hair, he slipped the other down her shoulder, to the curve of her waist, hips, the juncture of her thighs. She gasped against his mouth, a small, needy, throaty sound that drove him wild.

Desire, fierce and hot, burst inside him. He wanted her.

Her.

He opened his eyes, shock pouring through him as he jerked to full waking awareness with the realization that the woman in his dream wasn't Rebecca.

He didn't want Rebecca.

He wanted the woman in his arms who was staring back at him with equal startlement.

And she was no dream.

"What the hell are you doing?"

Brade's voice was unbearably hoarse. Melissa, struck dumb for the first time in her life, could only blink at him in the moonlight and shadows for a full minute, her heart thumping out of control against the wall of her chest.

Her lips felt tender and her head felt woozy, and her entire body tingled with sensual awareness.

He shoved off her, and she could breathe again. She barely made out his expression, but he looked horrified, disgusted.

Anger coursed through her, giving her back her voice.

"What am I doing?" she hurled at him, scrambling to a sitting position. He was blocking the entrance to the tent. She wanted out, now. "You were the one doing the kissing, buster. What the hell were *you* doing?''

She'd kissed him back, but that wasn't the point. That was a humiliating lapse she preferred to omit.

"You promised me you wouldn't touch me!" she charged, grasping at anything she could use against him. Obviously, self-restraint wasn't working. She needed additional ammunition.

"You're in my tent!" he bellowed back.

She noticed the uneven pull of his breath and a traitorous female satisfaction poured through her. He might be mad that he'd kissed her. He might even be disgusted that he'd kissed her. But he'd wanted her.

He'd desired her.

The knowledge was alarming and . . . thrilling . . . at the same time. What was going on here?

She had no idea what had just happened. She'd been picking his pocket one second, and the next he'd been sucking her tongue into his mouth—and she'd been so shocked, she'd let him.

She wasn't sure if it had been curiosity, or something more appalling. She just wished she could forget it.

But her lips were still wet and trembly with the memory. Nope, she wasn't forgetting it. Not in this lifetime.

He'd been good, really good. She'd never been kissed like that before, as if a man were eating her alive—and she was just as hungry, feeding on him in return.

Even now, her nipples tightened just looking at him. How could he do that to her?

Who did he think he was?

"Your tent! What does that mean?" she blasted him with all the frustrated yearning inside her. It wasn't curiosity, she knew sharply. It was—lust! She was lusting after *him!* How long had that been going on? Maybe since the first second she'd seen him, she thought with horror. The realization made her that much angrier. She'd liked it better when she just thought he desired her. Her desiring him was worse, much worse. "Do you think you have a right to maul every woman who pokes her head inside your tent?"

"I didn't maul you."

"No, you— You k-k—" He had her stuttering again!

In the shadows, his body now blocking both the opening of the tent and the moonlight, she couldn't see anything but the hot look in his eyes, which unnerved her even more than his kisses.

"What were you doing in my tent?" he demanded, his voice quiet but somehow more scary than when he was bellowing.

She sensed he didn't want to discuss the fact that they'd been kissing any more than she did.

Not that discussing what she was really doing in his tent would be any better. Her head spun, still stupidly fuzzy.

"I had to go to the bathroom," she said quickly. "You know, behind that nice rock you provided me," she added dryly. "I guess I got turned around coming back. I thought this was my tent."

"It's not."

"Well, thanks for the news flash!"

He glared at her across the short distance which separated them.

"Get out," he said, his voice dangerous.

"I would, but you're in my way."

He pushed out of the tent, and stomped several feet away, facing the cove. She crawled out after him, skirting his hard, angry body and heading straight for the relative safety of her own tent.

She'd nearly had the radio wire. But she'd lost it, and there was no way she was going back for it again.

Not with big, bad Brade and his hot, hungry lips waiting for her.

She couldn't risk going back in there.

What had that kiss been about? Obviously, he hadn't been completely awake, but he must have been having some pretty erotic dreams to kiss her that way.

What really bugged her was how repulsed he'd acted when it was over. She wasn't ugly. What was his problem? First he'd kissed her, then he'd acted as if she was a carrier for a deadly new plague.

The most humiliating thing was that she hadn't even resisted him! *He* was the one who'd stopped the kiss—not her!

This weekend couldn't get worse, Melissa decided.

That was when the sticks she'd jerry-rigged her tent with decided to give way, and a mass of canvas fell down on top of her head.

Brade stirred the gloppy mixture of buckwheat groats, oat flakes, dry milk powder and water in a metal pot he'd set up over the firepit. He tried not to look at the woman sleeping a few feet away, her limbs stretched out in every direction on top of her air mattress, her tent nothing but a heap of canvas at her feet.

He'd seen it come down on her last night, and would have helped her, but the idea of getting anywhere close to her after the incident in his tent had held him back.

He didn't trust himself near her. And besides, he had his doubts about whether she would have let him help her, anyway. She'd been pretty angry last night— and so had he. More angry at himself than at her, to be honest.

But who was being honest?

He stirred the pot of mush. Honesty wasn't going to get him anywhere at the moment. Not when it came to the desire he felt for the loony, irritating, much too sexy woman he was trapped with on Half Moon.

She stretched and turned over, flipping off the narrow air mattress and landing face first in the sand. She half-coughed, half-choked and pushed up to a sitting position. Blinking, she streaked her palms over her face, then rubbed her eyes. She noticed him then. Framed by the disheveled mess of her hair, she glared at him, her dark eyes sultry, her thick lashes flecked with sand. The bright morning sunlight lit up her golden tresses, framing her with a misleadingly angelic aura.

"I hate you," she greeted him sullenly.

"Good morning to you, too," he said, determined to remain unmoved by anything she said or did. He nodded toward the pot bubbling over the firepit. If he was going to remain unmoved, looking at her wasn't a smart move. All he could think about when he looked at her were those succulent lips of hers and how she'd tasted last night. . . . He needed to get his mind on something else, fast. "Mush?" he inquired stoically.

She pounced to her feet and began brushing off her shorts, and Brade tried not to remember how the curve of her hips had felt in his hands last night.

He wasn't sure he believed her story about how she'd ended up in his tent, but it didn't matter. He had to get control of the treacherous heat that boiled up every time he looked at her.

Mush. He forced his mind back to the mush. Plain, tasteless, good-for-you mush.

"No. I don't want any mush. I don't eat mush for breakfast. I could go for some toaster waffles, though. Got any? I'll take mine with strawberry syrup."

She stomped right up to him and he had to look

at her. All thoughts of mush evaporated from his mind. Awareness stabbed him. Her T-shirt had slipped off one shoulder in her sleep, revealing a creamy expanse of skin. Soft, warm skin he'd touched last night. . . .

Suddenly, the morning air felt hot and thick.

"Take me home," she demanded.

"Tomorrow." *An eternity,* he thought to himself. Far too long. It occurred to him that it was a good thing she stunk right now. The combination of too much bug spray and a long hot night hadn't done her any favors. "Go take a shower," he suggested, biting the inside of his mouth to keep from laughing when her eyes flashed with fury.

"Excuse me?"

"A shower. You know, the cleansing of the body." If looks could kill, he'd be six feet under.

"I'd be happy to take a shower," she said tightly. "But you've already informed me that you left the bathroom tent back in Charleston." She tipped her head and added a dose of false sweetness—a deadly dose of it—to her voice. "Perhaps now would be a good time to head back."

He thumbed toward the curve in the cove where the waterfall tumbled down between the rocks. The campfire was set up just around the slight bend, with enough thick foliage between to block the view from where they were standing.

He'd risen early—after catching nothing more than a second or two of sleep since the incident in his tent—and had already bathed and dressed long before dawn had fully broken over Half Moon. He'd started the fire in the pit and tried to pretend he was here alone.

But every time he almost convinced himself of it, she would stretch, yawn, groan or something, twisting and turning on her air mattress until that final time when she'd flipped herself over and woken herself up.

She was impossible to ignore.

"The shower's that way," he explained, hoping she'd take a nice, long one. Maybe for half the day.

"You've got to be kidding." She rolled her eyes. "What am I saying? You have no sense of humor." Turning, she went back and hefted the duffel bag containing her clothes and toiletries over her shoulder. "Fine. I can handle it. I refuse to be defeated. Or dirty."

She stalked off around the bend.

He watched her go. She was really hostile today. He wondered if it was because of that kiss, or if she just wasn't a morning person. Then he wondered what he was doing wondering. He had no interest in dissecting her flaky personality.

She didn't come back.

Brade ate his buckwheat mush alone, popping a few raisins in for sweetening, trying not to imagine what her lush body looked like naked . . . with water sluicing over it. He downed a cup of strong coffee from a tin pot he kept over the firepit, then another. He couldn't hear a thing except the standard accompaniment of surf, the cawing of birds, and the splash and trickle of the waterfall.

He'd wanted to be rid of her, but now that she'd been gone so long, he was starting to worry.

What if something had happened to her? What if she'd decided to go exploring and gotten lost, or fallen in a hole, or—

She wasn't a two-year-old, he reminded himself. She was a grown woman. A grown naked woman. A grown naked *angry* woman. If she caught him sneaking up on her at the waterfall, she might hit him over the head with a rock.

He waited another twenty minutes, threw his third cup of coffee on the fire, and went after her.

"Dagmar!" he hollered. No answer. "Melissa!" he tried. She was a loon. She might not answer to Dagmar. Or Melissa. Maybe she had a new name today.

She certainly wasn't answering. Nothing but surf and cawing and trickling. No "Leave me alone, you big dumb jerk," like he might expect to hear from her.

This weekend, he decided as he dragged in a deep breath and headed around the curve in the cove, was killing him. Coop was going to owe him, big time, for the rest of his life.

He pushed through the overhanging foliage and his heart nearly stopped.

She was dressed in clean clothes, lying on her side, little damp locks of hair curling around her fresh-scrubbed face. The rest of it hung in wet strands down her back, as she rested her head on her duffel with the mossy bank as her bed. Red berries—poisonous red berries—sat in an innocent pile beside her.

Brade sprinted the short distance to reach her, his heart in his throat. She was breathing, thank God. He didn't stop, didn't even think—he scooped her up and started running.

Chapter Eight

Melissa jerked to bewildered awareness—in Brade's arms. He was running hell-for-leather across the beach, and she felt every bouncing, heaving step.

Had the man gone mad?

She'd been taking a nice little nap, enjoying the first moment of complete peace and privacy since she'd arrived at this godforsaken island, when he'd suddenly swooped in, flung her over his shoulder as if he really were an action hero saving her from—

What could possibly threaten them on a deserted island? An army of lizards? An uprising of millipedes?

Pirates?

She lifted her head as he jostled her mercilessly.

Nope, no one-eyed, peg-legged maniacs chasing them down with flashing cutlasses.

There was just one maniac here—the one who had her flung over his shoulder like a sack of potatoes.

She pummelled his steel back, using both fists. "Put me down, you stupid jerk!"

He stopped short and the next thing she knew she was hitting the sand.

She stared at the big blue sky for a long beat, the air knocked out of her chest. Then Brade's dark, chiseled face blocked the light, and all she could see was his fierce face and those compelling eyes.

"You're okay?" he ground out.

She blinked. "Well, I was okay before you woke me up, hauled me halfway across the island and dropped me like a hot rock." She pushed up on her elbows, realizing they were all the way back up the beach.

Beyond him, she could see the plane. She looked at it longingly for a moment.

If there was one good thing that might come out of this hellish weekend, she thought briefly, it could be that she might get over her fear of flying. She wanted so desperately to get into that plane and take off that all her usual anxiety about flying—even just *thinking* about flying—had disappeared.

"You didn't eat the berries?"

Brade's question brought her attention back to his fuming face. A curious mixture of concern and wrath sharpened his already-hard features.

"Berries?" What was he talking about? "Oh, you mean those red berries? I was going to ask you about them. They looked delicious, but I didn't want to eat them without asking you if they were— Oh!"

Comprehension flashed through her mind.

"They're poisonous," he said.

"You thought I'd eaten them? What do you think I am, stupid?"

"You were lying there—"

"I was sleeping, you idiot! I had the worst possible night, and after I got cleaned up, I felt so tired that I just lay down on my duffel in the shade and—" More comprehension hit her.

She'd missed the best chance she might have all weekend!

He'd been about to take her to the plane! He'd thought she was going to die or something!

He was already getting up, brushing sand off his hands from where he'd crouched over her, and stomping off back down the beach to the cove.

"Wait!" she hollered after him. "I forgot! I *did* eat some of them!"

He kept right on walking, his muscular back rigid.

She took a dramatic pose, dropping from her half-raised position back onto the sand.

"Help!" she shouted. She took a sideways peek.

Brade was a tiny speck down the beach. He hadn't even looked back, not once. She pushed up on her elbows and gazed longingly at the plane again.

"Help," she whispered, and flopped back onto the sand again.

She discovered what the tide had done to her little rock arrangement overnight.

"Why didn't you tell me that was going to happen?" she demanded, stalking up to him where he sat, hunched, at the firepit, whittling angrily on a piece of wood with a silver knife.

Brade had been at the task ever since he'd made a fool of himself rushing her back to the plane.

He'd jumped to conclusions. He just couldn't be responsible for anything happening to her, that's all. It was guilt. It was Rebecca.

But it felt like more than that, and that was what had him in such a surly mood.

His sexy hostage was in a temper of her own. She had her fists planted on her trim hips and was glaring at him like a vengeful sorceress about to cast an evil spell.

Or maybe she'd already done that. There was *something* wrong with him, and bewitchment was as good an explanation as any.

She was all sparkly eyes and bouncy hair and curvy breasts. Or at least, that was all he saw when he looked at her, anyway.

Whittle, he told himself.

Focus.

He made another savage swipe at the wood, concentrating on the tiny flying chips falling between his feet and the miniature totem taking shape in his hands.

The miniature totem that had . . . breasts!

He swore ripely, the simmering boil he was trying to keep down rising relentlessly to the surface. Tossing the carving into the fire, he glowered at her.

"You didn't ask my advice," he said flatly.

Her furious sniff almost made him laugh, but he was in too much of a bad mood.

"You could have—" She clamped her lips tight for a long beat.

She stared out at the water, and her dark eyes narrowed.

He followed her gaze, seeing what she saw. A big fishing boat was trawling offshore.

She started jumping up and down, waving and hollering. There was no sign of acknowledgment from the boat.

Her chest heaving, she glared at him again.

"See that?" She pointed out to sea. "I'm getting out of here. Today. So, this is good-bye."

He tipped his head, regarding her. What did she have planned now?

Was she going to swim out to the boat? It was far, way too far, to swim. Unless she was an Olympic competitor. And he doubted that.

No, she had to have something else in mind.

He tamped down his curiosity. Whatever she was

going to do, it wouldn't work. The fishing boat was headed out to sea. She'd never get their attention.

"Bye," he told her.

She flipped around and tromped up the beach, gazed out at the boat for a contemplative moment, tapping one foot, her arms crossed tightly over her chest. Then she flipped around again and made a beeline for the jungle.

He watched as, staying just within the first few feet of jungle, she hauled one fallen tree limb after another down to the beach. They were sizeable limbs.

Was she planning to use them to brain him over the head next time he fell asleep?

Then she started pulling down some of the grapevines that hung from every tree. Her face was a mask of concentration, even from a distance. She didn't look back at him, not once. Just kept hauling and piling, hauling and piling.

She was quite industrious.

He grabbed another piece of wood from the burnpile and started whittling again. Maybe she was going to build a signal fire. That sounded like the kind of batty idea she'd come up with. He wasn't going to worry about it. He'd had enough of her for one morning.

The fishing boat was getting smaller and smaller as it headed toward the horizon.

When he looked up from his carving some time later, he saw her wrapping the big sticks together with the thick vines.

That was when he realized she was building a raft. She was going to try to sail out to the fishing boat!

In fact, she was nearly ready. As he watched, she wrapped the last vine around the last tree limb and pushed the ridiculous contraption into the surf.

Brade got to his feet.

For a wild beat, he wondered if her scheme was actually going to work. Surely she wasn't really going to try this.

It would never work.

It was too far.

She'd couldn't possibly make it to the fishing boat, and there was no way of knowing if anyone aboard would see her and help. She could drown.

Unless the raft floated.

But that was impossible. Anyone with half a brain could see that.

Unless a person was desperate and determined. Not to mention batty, totally batty.

She yanked the raft into knee-deep water, and it was still floating. She climbed aboard and started paddling out to sea.

Brade started running.

She made it to the first line of breakers—they were small ones, and she rolled right after them. Luckily for her, the relentless, pounding surf didn't rise to dangerous swells unless it was high tide.

Looking back at him where he'd stopped at the shoreline, she swung her hand in a Miss America parade wave. Brade thought for a second she was actually going to make it.

Damnation! Her crazy plan was going to work—

Then the raft sank.

Chapter Nine

Melissa came up spitting seawater, flapping her arms, blinking water out of her eyes as she searched for the fishing boat. Surely they'd see her, come rushing to her rescue—

But all she could see was a dark speck on the horizon. Her heart sank as deep as her raft. She flapped her arms some more, treading water.

She was going to have to go back to shore. Back to Brade. *This is all his fault,* she fumed.

He'd hijacked her.

He'd kept her in this tropical Hades against her will.

He'd forced her to concoct all these stupid escape plans.

Melissa gave herself permission to waste her precious energy cursing his black heart. She was a good swimmer, and she wasn't that far offshore. She could stay out here for . . . another couple of minutes while she mapped her next move.

There were always the berries, she recalled. She could just eat them. That was one sure way to get him to take her back to Charleston.

Of course, the berries could kill her. That was a snag.

Better *he* eat the berries. She enjoyed a moment of satisfaction. She imagined herself attending his funeral wake, reading his eulogy.

He was a good kidnapper, she would begin. . . .

She laughed, then paid for it when a low swell rolled over her head. She swallowed a mouthful of water, and came up sputtering and remembering that if he ate the berries, there wouldn't be anyone to fly her back home.

She could get the radio wire from him and call for help— But she wasn't positive she could reconnect it, and if he was dead, she'd be stuck.

How would she get him to eat the berries, anyway? Another snag.

No, she needed a plan that didn't involve killing him. Unfortunately, she didn't have one. All her fantasies at the moment involved Brade and major bodily damage.

Still treading water, she narrowed her gaze on the island and wondered where he was now. She couldn't see a soul on the island. Then she saw *something* racing through the water, heading straight for her.

"Oh, my God," she breathed.

Were there sharks around here?

She didn't have the slightest idea. But she liked her limbs right where they were—attached to her body. So she started plowing back to shore, adrenaline pumping her arms and legs all the faster.

Then she felt *something* brush her arm.

She screamed, inhaling water, and spit and spewed as she kept hauling toward shore.

Then *something* grabbed her, pulled her into a liquid embrace. She screamed again, flailing and pushing and whacking with her arms and legs.

It wasn't a shark.

She blinked through the droplets of water sticking to her lashes. Oh my God, she thought, stunned.

She was being attacked by Aqua Man.

"I've got you," Brade said, holding her around the waist, pulling her as he started swimming. With every hard, long, heaving stroke, he dragged her under, then up, under, then up.

She tried to get away, but he had a death grip on her.

"I've got myself!" she sputtered between strokes. "Let me—"

She went under again.

"I don't need—" She tried when she came back

up, but a second later she was drinking saltwater for her efforts.

He is going to drown me.

Then she felt her toes scraping sandy bottom, but her rescuer wasn't done. He kept hauling her, with her fighting him all the way, straight up the shore till they hit dry beach.

He put her down with a whomp on the sand.

"Are you all right?" Brade asked, peering over her. Water sluiced down his dark, hard features. His T-shirt was plastered to every corrugated muscle of his shoulders, arms and chest.

He was so gorgeous. It was criminal for a man to look that good.

Melissa stared at him for a timeless beat and wondered if maybe it wouldn't be so bad if she just went ahead and killed him. He deserved it—for being irresistible, if nothing else.

She'd be trapped on Half Moon for the rest of her life, alone, but maybe it was a fitting punishment for lusting after such a barbarian.

"Oh yeah, I'm just fine, thanks to you," she snapped. She pushed him out of the way, scrambled to her feet, and stepped right into a hole.

Brade scooped her into his arms before she could fall. Hadn't they just been through this scenario? he thought. But he couldn't let anything happen to her.

Not on his watch.

She might be a kook. She might be a pain in the neck.

But she had to make it through this weekend alive—even if it killed her.

"What are you doing?" She socked him in the chest with her free fist, her other hand smashed against his chest. "Put me down," she commanded. "I can walk, you dolt. I can swim, too, by the way."

She thrashed and kicked for all she was worth, but they were already at the firepit. He plopped her down on the sand again.

"Here." He grabbed her sleeping bag and wrapped it around her soaked shoulders. He dished up some of the leftover mush in a bowl and pushed it at her quickly. "Eat this."

She took a look at the tepid concoction. "You want me to be sick?" She pushed the bowl back at him. "I'm not eating that. What's your problem, anyway?"

"You collapsed. It was probably the strain of all that swimming plus the work you did this morning hauling wood down to the beach. You need some food."

"I didn't collapse—I tripped in a hole!" she bellowed at him, her dark eyes flashing. "And I was fine when I was in the ocean, by the way. I was fine when I was sleeping by the waterfall, too. Why do you keep trying to rescue me? Do you have some kind of superhero complex or what? Next time, wait for the Bat signal before you come running."

"I'm responsible for your safety," he ground out.

She was making him feel like an idiot. She was right—why did he keep overreacting? It was as if he actually cared or something!

"I'm perfectly capable of being responsible for my own safety, thank you very much," she ranted on. "All I want you to do is take me back to Charleston! And I don't want this sleeping bag on me! Are you trying to give me heatstroke?" She pushed off the offending sleeping bag, tossing it into a heap dangerously close to the smoldering firepit. "It's eighty degrees out here."

She jumped to her feet.

Brade's gaze glued to her wet chest. Her full breasts bobbed and jiggled, her nipples poking against the thin material.

And her dark-rose nipples could be clearly seen through the soaked white cotton.

"What the hell do you think you're doing?" he breathed hoarsely.

She blinked, following his gaze to glance down at her chest. The flush of her cheeks deepened visibly, but she didn't do anything about the situation except to lift her chin higher.

"You're not wearing anything under that shirt," he barked. "What are you, an exhibitionist?"

She huffed furiously. "Excuse me. I didn't know I was going to get wet today. It's too hot to wear a bra out here and—"

He lobbed her duffel bag at her. "Get some dry clothes on. Now."

Her eyes narrowed and she crossed her arms over her chest, only managing to push those plump, pointy mounds together and make him that much more angry.

"What's the rush?" she inquired. "You know, actually, this wet T-shirt kind of feels good in this heat. I think I might wear it this way till it dries. Got a problem with that?"

She was baiting him, and he knew it. His jaw flexed and he tried to control the savage desire he didn't want to feel. She had no idea she was teasing a man who hadn't had sex in five years.

"If you don't have dry clothes on by the time I count to three—"

"You'll what?"

"Don't push me," he warned softly, the lowering of his tone only making it that much more dangerous. "I make the rules around here, and you staying properly dressed is one of them. I already told you that. Now get changed."

Her beautiful, defiant expression wavered only a little, but she just tilted her chin higher. She was as angry as he was, and completely unstoppable.

"What are you going to do?" she inquired hotly. "Spank me? Tie me up? Feed me mush? Kiss me again?"

His heart beat hard and heavy against the wall of his chest. She looked as shocked at the words that had come out of her mouth as he was.

She took an instinctive step back.

He reached out and reeled her in like a hooked fish. He wanted to throw her over his shoulder and fly her back to Charleston, now, before things got worse.

But he didn't. He couldn't. So things got worse.

Chapter Ten

Melissa should have known better.

A little voice had told her to beware of him from the second she'd laid eyes on him. But the longer she spent in his company, the less she was listening to her little voice. There was something about him that made her keep pushing forward instead of backing down.

Provoking him was crazy, but she'd done it, and now she had to live with the consequences. Brade had kissed her before. She knew what was coming.

She was ready.

No big deal.

A breath caught in her throat, and she lowered

her lashes, swaying on the tiptoes she hadn't even realized she'd been standing on—the tiptoes that made it that much easier for him to crush her to him, his arms locking around her waist.

He slashed his mouth across hers, pushing his tongue inside in a full-out assault that she returned, plunder for plunder. He tasted like wild passion and unrealized need, and she didn't even know when she hooked her leg around him—only knew she'd done it when she felt the swollen rise of his erection.

But even that didn't stop her—or him.

They kept kissing, lost in a passionate frenzy of desire, completely out of control.

He could take her right there, on the sand. In fact, the one leg she was still standing on was buckling already. It wouldn't take a feather to push her down—

Her own throaty moan brought her back to sanity.

What was she thinking?

"Stop!" she cried against his mouth, hammering at his chest and shoulders.

She was appalled by her body's insane, instinctive reactions to him.

He let go of her instantly, and she almost lost her balance as she set her other foot back down. When she finally steadied herself and looked at his face, ready to blast him some more, she was shocked.

There was nothing hidden in his expression now, no shadows, no hooded secrets. Suddenly, she saw the real Brade, the one he didn't want the world to see. The one she'd only caught glimpses of before.

The look of vulnerable need in his eyes reduced her to nothing more than a sweet, savage emotional response.

She reached out to him again, feeling touched and compelled—to what, she wasn't even sure. She just knew it wasn't a game anymore.

It wasn't some crazy battle.

This was life and death and everything in between. She felt connected to him, in some way she didn't fully understand.

"What," she breathed, too dumbfounded to say anything else, "was that?"

His gaze shuttered, his jaw hardened. The real Brade was gone, vanished, just like that.

"Nothing. It was nothing." His breathing was uneven, and his voice was rough, grating. "Now get your clothes changed. From now on, you do what I say, when I say it. Got that?"

Melissa swallowed hard. What had just happened here?

He might be blowing it off, but she didn't believe him for a minute when he said it was nothing. That kiss had been *something*—fire and fury and some kind of pain that was elemental and deep and connected them, body and soul.

And now he was going to just go straight back to barking at her!

"You kissed me," she said, stuck on that point and not moving. "You kissed me twice."

"I'm a man," he ground out harshly. "You're a

walking wet T-shirt contest." He scowled at her. "I said, get changed. Now."

He wheeled away from her.

That was it. He'd just kissed her, for the second time, and was going to act—again!—as if it were the most digusting thing that had ever happened to him.

Under normal circumstances, this situation would never have happened. She was usually practical, reserved, modest.

What was happening to her?

Brade.

She'd spent most of her adult life staving off men's advances. It wasn't that she had some cherished ideals about her virginity. She wasn't saving herself. She'd just never met a man who was the slightest bit tempting.

She was picky—absurdly so, Dagmar would say. But she had her reasons. Reasons all tied up in a pain and fear that had stalked her from childhood and that Dagmar understood even though she pretended not to.

Dagmar had her own pain, her own fear, and Melissa knew that as well. It explained Dagmar's relationship with Coop. Which was what had gotten Melissa in this fix, she remembered with irritation.

She glared at Brade.

How had he done it—broken through, tempted her, touched her?

And how dare he just ... walk away and call it nothing! It was *not* nothing!

"Or what?" she shouted after him, pushing forward again instead of backing down, driven by that strange connection she'd felt with him for that timeless beat, and by anger and bewilderment ... and hurt.

She felt hurt.

And that just made her angrier.

She strode up to him, sand flying from her heels, and whirled in front of him, planting herself smack in his path and forcing him to stop.

"What are you going to do now?" she demanded, fists set firmly on her hips. "You've already kissed me—twice! That's the vilest torture I can think of."

She was lying through her teeth and could only pray he wouldn't know it.

"What can you possibly do to me that's worse than that?" she went on. "Nothing," she answered her own question. "You can do nothing. You can keep me on this island all weekend, but you can't control me. I'll walk around naked if I want to. And if that makes you mad, well, too bad!"

The coldness of the look he leveled on her made her shiver in the eighty-degree sun.

"I can get in that plane and leave you here," he promised grimly.

Melissa's breath jammed in her throat.

He stepped just to the left, stomped around her

and on up the beach, and she didn't say another word.

Brade stalked halfway up the island, fueled by anger and something else he didn't want to name, before he stopped. He wasn't heading for the plane—but in the opposite direction entirely.

Despite what he'd said to his beautiful captive, he'd never fly off and leave her alone on Half Moon Island.

But he still needed to get away from her, away from her beautiful breasts and her fearless, fascinating mouth, and all the unwelcome, unallowable emotions she evoked in him.

He stopped at the point, the tip of the crescent-shaped island, and sat down on the rocky promontory there. The beach was rough and narrow here, mostly cliff and scruffy grass.

But he couldn't get away from her, even though she didn't follow. It was that wounded shadow that his harsh words had placed in her eyes that he couldn't shake.

What right did she have to look hurt?

No right at all, he answered his own question.

She was the one who'd provoked him. So why was he feeling guilty?

Because she touched something dark and empty inside him. Because when he kissed her, she made him think he could be whole again.

That something he didn't want to name twisted inside him.

How could she do this to him?

Everything he'd been told about Dagmar Parker had prepared him to despise her—especially that she was selfish, vain, erratic. But the woman he knew here on Half Moon was strong and courageous and spirited, and he respected her in spite of himself.

And he owed her an apology.

He didn't want to do it, but he had no choice— because if he didn't do it, that dark and empty part of him was going to swallow him up.

Arriving back at the camp an hour later, he found her dressed in fresh clothes, stabbing the fishing spear at the water. He'd heard her swearing for a good five minutes before she came into view.

He needed a shower himself. His clothes were stiff and crusty from saltwater and from the sun that had dried them to his skin.

But she needed him more.

He knew she had to be starving, and he knew, too, that she would rather ask a rattler to bite her on her sexy bottom than ask him for help.

"What are you doing?" Melissa reeled around in midcurse, dropping her fishing spear in the glittering shallow water of the cove.

Brade's face was close, too close.

"You need help."

"No, I don't," she said snappishly.

She'd eat those poisonous berries before she ate a fish he caught for her.

"Yes, you do," he persisted. "Come on. I saw the Bat signal."

One of his dark brows spiked and she could have sworn his eyes sparkled.

What was this?

Had he had a sense of humor implanted in the last thirty minutes?

She drew away from him. She couldn't think with his arms around her. When he was near, her pulse quickened and something uncomfortably sexual stirred within her.

This was why she'd never had sex before, she understood suddenly.

Other men had sparked her interest, but none had evoked this aching physical longing . . . and the grip on her heart that made her chest feel tight and anxious.

He made her feel as if she had to either have sex with him, or die. And she hated him for that.

"I figured you'd be halfway back to Charleston by now," she said archly.

He studied her. He looked oddly wary.

"I owe you an apology," he said, his words simple and direct, wasting no time. "I shouldn't have threatened to leave you here alone. I want you to know that I would never do that."

So that was it, she thought. He felt guilty. She wasn't letting him off that easy.

"It's not necessary," she said tensely. "What is this, kidnappers' code of ethics all of a sudden?" She bent down, stretched for the spear in the water, taking hold of it with the tip of one finger and dragging it back to shore. "Bug off, Brade."

She stalked up the cove with the spear, trying to focus on the few fish she could see swimming along.

"All right," he said, his voice coming from far enough behind her that she knew he hadn't moved. "I was going to offer you some cookies as a truce, but I guess I'll just eat them by myself."

Melissa dropped the spear and wheeled.

Cookies?

He was still standing where she'd left him. There he was, all tough-guy glamor and screen-god looks.

And she was going to kill him if he was tricking her now.

"No way," she said, suspicious. "You're a health nut. That stuff'll kill you. That's what you said."

He shrugged those big, powerful shoulders.

"Coop told me what a cookie fanatic you are," he explained. "I thought I'd grab a bag, that maybe they'd come in handy at some point. They're your favorite," he went on. "Double chocolate-chip chunk. With nuts. From the Dover Street Bakery."

Those were Dagmar's favorite cookies from her favorite bakeshop. They weren't Melissa's favorite, but this wasn't the place to be picky.

Her mouth watered and her knees felt like jelly. She almost felt dizzy.

She was starving!

And he had cookies!

She narrowed her gaze on him. "If you're lying to me—"

"You'll what?" he tossed her own attitude back at her. His mouth curled into something that almost resembled a smile.

"I'll make sure you don't live long enough to fly out of here—with me or without me," she said with not a quibble of conscience.

She advanced on him.

"Where are they?"

"In my duffel," he said.

She turned and ran straight for it. She'd been afraid to search the bag yesterday; and today, she'd been so busy being mad at him, she'd forgotten about it completely.

A herd of stampeding elephants couldn't keep her out of it now.

She had her finger on the flap of his duffel when his hard, powerful hand clamped down over hers.

"Just one thing."

"What?" she almost screamed at him in desperation. She was going to bite his hand if he didn't give her those cookies in two more seconds.

"We call a truce," he explained. "No more escaping. No more rafts. No more rocks. No more sneaking into my tent in the middle of the night to get the radio wire."

So he hadn't bought her spur-of-the-moment story about getting lost coming back from the bathroom. This didn't surprise her.

"Whatever." She tried to push his hand away, but he wasn't budging.

"Say it and mean it."

His cool eyes burned through her and she had no choice. She lied.

Chapter Eleven

"I will not try to escape again," she said obediently.

Brade didn't believe her. She was lying. But she was also hungry, so he moved his hand.

She ripped open his duffel and plunged her hand inside, seizing the white bakery bag. Her face lit up like a little girl discovering a dollhouse under the tree on Christmas morning.

Brade sat down on a log by the campfire and watched her dive into the bag without the slightest evidence of self-consciousness. He thought back to the woman who'd stepped out of that taxi at Fortin Airfield and walked across the tarmac to his plane.

He hadn't liked that woman, aside from what he'd

already known about Dagmar Parker. She'd been too well-groomed and sophisticated. Too perfect.

The woman she'd become in the last twenty-four hours was more interesting. More real. She wasn't flawlessly groomed now, but she was still beautiful, even without makeup. In fact, she was more beautiful.

And she wasn't sophisticated, either—instead she was earthy and exciting.

What would happen when she went back? he wondered suddenly, then next he wondered why he cared. He wouldn't see her again.

The knowledge bothered him for some stupid reason. It was painful and weird.

There was a rawness to what he was feeling, as if he were opening an old wound. He couldn't deny what was happening, the painful need building inside him, but he could control it. He'd have to.

And yet his body hummed with expectancy, preparing for some physical event. Hot sparks zinged off every nerve end in his body when he looked at her.

He didn't want to think about what sex with her would be like, but he couldn't stop. Why was she the one woman in all these years who tempted him? He'd had plenty of chances. There were always women ready to throw themselves at the scion of the Cox Toys fortune.

But he hadn't been the least bit tempted by a single one. 'Til now—and this woman didn't even know who he was and was hardly throwing herself at him.

He jerked to his feet.

"I'm going to get cleaned up," Brade announced abruptly and headed for the waterfall. He prayed the water would be cold.

Melissa watched him go. She had a cookie stuffed in her mouth, and was trying to resist plowing the whole bag in at once.

The cookies were delicious. Junk food of the gods.

She wondered why he was being so nice all of a sudden. Guilt? Or something else? What was this truce really about? The last twenty-four hours seemed like years—and yet she didn't know the man she'd spent them with at all.

But she felt connected to him just the same. It was strange and inexplicable.

She crunched the top of the bag together, frustrated, and pushed it back into his duffel. Suddenly, accepting favors from Brade didn't seem like a good idea. She didn't know where this whole thing was leading, she just knew she was still here on this island—and she was a little bit afraid of what was going to happen next.

She was starting to actually like the man. It made no sense, but there it was. He made her feel hot and breathless, consumed by something that she feared could burn her up if she wasn't careful.

The truce was a bad thing, and she had no intention of holding to her words. Unfortunately, she was fresh out of escape schemes.

She walked down the beach, sat down, hunching her arms over her knees, and stared out at the water moodily. She was stuck on Half Moon.

And the hell of it was, right then, she wasn't sure she minded. She was tired of trying to escape, tired of fighting. She didn't like giving up, but what else could she do right now? And she had to admit, the place was a tropical paradise, if she troubled to take a good look, and Brade wasn't exactly hard on the eyes, either.

She squeezed her eyes shut, let out a frustrated moan, and dropped back on the sand. A crisp breeze blew over her sizzling skin. She had to do something. Giving up was dangerous. She had to get out of here, before—

"You'll get sunburned."

Melissa opened her eyes, shading them from the sun with her hand, squinting to see Brade standing over her all fresh and clean and superhero-ish.

Oh, man. She could feel her heart go flutter-flutter, pitter-patter.

"So what," she said sullenly, annoyed at him all over again for being so good-looking.

"So put on some sunscreen," he said, and dropped a plastic bottle next to her.

She pushed up on her elbows. "Thanks," she said, surprised. "Aren't you thoughtful," she added warily.

He stared at her with his inscrutable eyes, didn't say anything.

She took the bottle and squirted some lotion into

her palm. "Are you going to sit down?" she asked. "Or are you going to stand there looming over me all day? Because you're blocking my sun."

He hunkered down beside her. She made a big job out of rubbing the coconut-smelling lotion over her arms.

She imagined him rubbing lotion over her arms and legs and other portions of her body. But he didn't offer, and she tossed the bottle back at him, irritated with herself for coming up with such a dumb fantasy. As if she would let him rub lotion on her! She'd stuff the bottle down his throat first.

"Why are you doing this?" she demanded by way of distraction.

"I don't want you to get sunburned."

"No, I mean this whole weekend. You're going to a lot of trouble to save somebody else's wedding."

The subject had come out of nowhere, but she was truly intrigued. She'd been too busy trying to escape to examine the man holding her hostage, but she had questions, lots of them.

Brade shrugged. "Coop's a good friend," he said simply. "I owe him."

"Why? What crime did he commit for you? Armed robbery? Grand larceny?"

He regarded her levelly, that riveting hint of a smile playing at his hard lips again.

"This isn't a crime," he reminded her. "It's engine trouble."

Melissa rolled her eyes. "Oh, yeah. I forgot."

"How long have you been afraid of flying?"

His question took her by surprise.

"I'm not afraid of flying," she returned in automatic fashion.

He stared at her for a long beat.

"Come on." He got to his feet, stretched out his hand to her.

She stared at his hand suspiciously.

What now? But she took it, curiosity stronger than leeriness. She was just bored, she told herself. Otherwise she wouldn't give him the time of day.

He dropped his grip on her hand as soon as she stood, and headed for the camp. He tucked the sunscreen back in his duffel when they got there and grabbed his shoes.

"Get yours," he told her.

Melissa didn't know if he meant her strappy sandals or the too-small watershoes; but she figured the sandals weren't good for anything out here, so she grabbed the pink and purple watershoes.

He headed back up the beach, and she ran to catch up with him. It took her a couple of minutes to realize they were heading for the plane.

"Oh my God," she breathed. "You're taking me home!"

He gave her a look that told her he'd just dropped his valuation of her brainpower by at least fifty percent.

"No. I'm taking you for a ride."

She stopped short.

"In the plane?"

"Of course."

"Why?"

"I'm going to let you fly it. For a few minutes."

She stared at him, dumbfounded. Her heart pumped. She was starting to feel sick already. She didn't like flying, but at least she could close her eyes most of the time, and try to pretend she was somewhere else—like on the ground.

The idea of having hold of the controls made her feel as if she was going to have a panic attack.

"Thanks, but no thanks," she said firmly. "Besides,"—she latched onto the first thing she thought of—"you're having engine trouble." She crossed her arms, backed away a few steps.

"I've been working on it," he said, taking hold of one of her upper arms and guiding her on toward the plane. His touch was gentle, but demanding. "I think we should take a test flight before tomorrow. And you're going to be my copilot."

"I don't th-think so," she argued even as she felt her traitorously limp knees letting him pull her forward.

She was too wigged out to even get mad at him for making her stutter again.

What was this flying thing, some new brand of torture? She couldn't believe he actually cared about her flying phobia. Why would he?

"Most of the time, people are afraid of the unknown," he said. "The unfamiliar. Things they don't understand or feel they have no control over."

Her gaze zipped to his chiseled face. That explained it, she thought a little dizzily. He'd just explained why she was afraid of him.

But flying was another thing altogether.

He still gripped her arm, which kept her from either running or fainting, she wasn't sure which.

"The first thing any pilot does is a good pre-flight check. A walk around the plane."

He kept talking, and her jellied knees kept supporting her as he directed her on an inspection of the small aircraft. She didn't take in half of what he was telling her. Her head was buzzing. She didn't want to get into that plane.

If he was going to take her home, fine. She'd be brave, keep her eyes shut the whole way back, and kiss the ground when they got there.

But his plans were quite different.

She felt sick, and she contemplated throwing up on his shoes. Did he really think she was going to keep her eyes open long enough up in the air to participate in controlling the plane?

"The lift an airplane needs to fly is produced by the wings," he was explaining. "Air molecules flowing over the top have to go farther to rejoin the air flowing underneath, and that causes the air to thin out and speed up. This creates a partial vacuum—and the lift that generates flight. It's science, not magic—so it's nothing to fear.''

He opened the hatch.

She scrunched her pinched feet in the too-small shoes, gripping the runway tarmac with her plastic soles. She felt as if something inside her was shrieking as loud as a fire alarm.

Any idea she'd had earlier that her desire to get back to Charleston might be diminishing her fear of flying vanished. Her fear was real and strong, taking her straight back to the past.

Her tongue felt thick and for a second she thought she was going to pass out.

Then she saw him reaching into his back pocket.

The radio wire!

Her dizzied brain sprang to alert. This could be her chance.

She took a deep breath, and another, swallowing back panic.

All he had to do was plug that radio wire in, and all she had to do was wait for him to be distracted and she could grab it, call for help and be rescued in no time.

If she could keep her eyes open.

"Well?" Brade prompted. "I'm not going to force you. If you're too scared—''

"No!" she cried quickly. "I think it s-sounds"—
she dragged in a harsh breath and tried to talk
slower—"like a good idea." She forced a perky, fake
smile. "Not that I'm scared of flying," she added,
just barely managing not to stutter. "Because I'm
not. But I've never had a chance to actually take the
controls before. Why not. Let's go." She was babbling,
but she couldn't help it. She was just glad she wasn't
throwing up.

He narrowed his gaze.

She climbed into the plane.

Yesterday, she hadn't paid much attention to the
copilot controls in the two-seater plane. She'd had
her eyes shut most of the way over, anyway.

She pretended to pay attention now, battling to
focus and keep her anxiety attack at bay. If she was
going to use this chance to its fullest potential, she
was going to have to keep her wits about her.

Brade started explaining the array of controls and
gauges. It mostly went over her head: air speed indica-
tor, altimeter, directional gyro, fuel gauge, and about
a zillion other things. Did he really think she was
going to remember any of it?

"Strap in," he said when he finished.

Her hands shook as she clicked the safety belt in
place.

She watched him reconnect the radio wire and put
on a headset mike, then flip a switch on the radio.

Adrenaline shot through her bloodstream as he

eased out the throttle, his intense gaze concentrated in that moment on the plane's control panel.

The airplane started rolling straight ahead, and he pushed the throttle all the way open.

She tore the headset off him.

"Help! I'm being held hostage on Half Moon Island—"

Chapter Twelve

Her outburst stumbled as Brade flicked her a glance. He eased back on the controls, lifting the nose of the aircraft.

Melissa's big dark eyes flashed desperation at his nonchalance, and she speeded up.

"—by Brade! Brade—something. With Cox Toys. He's crazy," she went on, her face transmitting a dozen emotions, fear, frustration, confusion chief among them. "He's—"

She broke off again.

"What's going on?" she demanded, her voice shaking. Her hands were shaking, too, as she pulled the headset down from her face. "Why aren't you stopping me? Why are you just—"

She flicked her gaze down to her lap, to the headset. "This isn't working, is it?"

He shook his head. "Do you think I was born yesterday?" He'd suspected she'd snatch it off his head and try to call for help, so he'd set it to a frequency he knew would be dead.

"I think you're certifiable!" she yelled at him. "I think you're—Oh, my God."

The plane took off.

She squeezed her eyes shut and her face turned so pale, for a second he considered touching back down. She was scared to death of airplanes, that much was clear. It made her vulnerable, yet even in that vulnerability she'd hatched another escape plot.

Brade had to respect her guts, and for that reason alone he was going to see if he couldn't help her overcome her flying phobia.

And that was the only reason, he told himself firmly.

Yet he found himself wondering if her fear of flying was in any way connected to the occasional stutters she tried so hard to control, and he had the terrible, painful idea that he was starting to care about her.

He forced himself to clear his mind, pushing away the unwelcome thoughts and feelings—refusing to deal with them now.

She'd dropped the headset, and he picked it back up. He doubted he'd need the radio. He'd plugged it in as a just-in-case measure but also because he'd figured the prospect of grabbing it would induce her to get into the airplane whether she wanted to or not.

He just hoped he was right about the rest of his plan.

"The primary flight controls are the control wheel and the rudder pedals," he said, making himself ignore her clenched eyelids and whitened knuckles. "They're connected to the moveable surfaces on the wings and tail by steel cables.

"When you push the wheel forward, the elevators on the tail are lowered, pulling the plane's tail up and pushing the nose down. Pull back and the elevators are raised, pulling the nose up.

"Turning the wheel to the right or left causes the plane to bank in the same direction."

They reached a cruising altitude over the ocean. The Atlantic shimmered in the bright sunshine.

He continued, explaining the concept of establishing a turn, and then maintaining it.

"Put your hands on the wheel."

She didn't move, though she did open her eyes and regard him fiercely. "I hate you."

Brade nodded. "Now we're getting somewhere. Put your hands on the wheel."

"Have you lost your mind?"

"Not yet," he said levelly, reaching over and hauling her left hand onto the wheel and keeping it there. "Though a few more hours with you could do the trick."

He winked at her, then wondered what the hell he was doing, flirting with her.

"I've already got one of my hands off the wheel," he said, focusing on the task at hand, getting his wayward thoughts in line. "If I have to take the other one off to put your other hand on the wheel, you'll be the only one flying the plane."

She slapped her right hand on the wheel lickety-split.

"Oh, what the heck." He took his other hand off the wheel. "I think you're ready to fly the plane, anyway."

Brade sat back, his body humming, prepared to resume control if necessary, but curious to see what she'd do under the circumstances.

If he knew his sexy captive, she'd rise to the occasion. He knew that. He just didn't think *she* did.

Melissa felt the vibration of the engine coming straight through her hands, and her mind spun. Below, Half Moon Island was a tiny scrap of lush green framed by brilliant beaches.

She wanted to tear her hands away and squeeze her eyes shut, but survival instinct—and something else—kept them in place.

Glancing at Brade, she saw the energy in his eyes, and some of that energy resonated in her. This was his world, and he loved it. His excitement was palpable.

"We're going to die," she said.

"No, we're not," he returned calmly. "Take it into a turn." He applied light pressure to her hands. "As you turn, you lose a little lift, so you have to add a little back pressure to the wheel to keep from losing altitude."

He placed his hands back on his own wheel, guiding her into the turn, and she barely noticed as he let her retake control a moment later—his movements and hers following seamlessly. The feel of the co-pilot's wheel rotating under her fingers, and the pedals moving under her feet, was weird and compelling.

She was actually affecting the movement of the plane!

Adrenaline poured through her system, and she was shocked to realize it wasn't so much anxiety as an incredible rush. Her heart beat loud in her ears, drowning out the noise of the cockpit, drowning out her fear.

She noticed Brade take his hands off the wheel, his aqua gaze studying her with some unreadable intensity.

"I'm flying," she shouted at him, a sense of control bursting over her.

She didn't want to throw up. She didn't want to shut her eyes. She didn't want this to ever end.

He nodded, and smiled at her.

Her heart flipped, and it was more than the exhilaration of flight.

"How do you know I won't fly us back to Charleston now?"

He laughed. "For one thing, if you keep on this course, you're going to take us to the Bahamas. For another, I'm not going to teach you to land."

Melissa couldn't help it, she laughed back at him. She was having a good time.

How dare he make her laugh!

But for the life of her, she couldn't rouse enough animosity to do anything but keep smiling as he took over, setting a course for Half Moon.

The plane touched down, and rolled to a stop.

Brade stuck the radio wire back into his pocket, but even that couldn't spoil Melissa's mood.

"I feel really good," she announced, climbing out of the plane after Brade.

Energy zipped and zinged wildly through her body. She wanted to dance, yell at the top of her lungs.

Kiss Brade.

That shook her up.

"Brade?"

"What?"

He didn't move, just stood there with the sun beating down between them. It was the middle of the afternoon. A pleasant breeze cut through the heat, carrying the fresh tang of salt.

"I still hate you," she said, grappling for the sense

of equilibrium that she seemed to have lost somewhere in the air.

Or maybe a long time before then, she realized. She was afraid the lack of balance she was feeling now had nothing to do with that flight.

He nodded. "I'd be disappointed if you didn't."

She licked her lips dryly. "Okay, well, just so we understand each other."

He nodded again. They stood there for another long beat.

All that zippy energy kept zinging.

She had to do something about it or she was going to be in trouble.

Reaching down, she slipped off the watershoes, dangling them from her fingertips. She gave him a look.

"Beat you to camp!" she blurted out, and waited a second to see if he'd take the challenge.

He did.

She dropped the shoes and tore down the sandy bank, to the beach and onward. She knew he'd catch up with her, and she waited until he was even with her and she staged a dramatic tumble.

He zoomed past her, spun, sand flying, and came huffing back.

"Are you all right?" He hunkered down, peering worriedly at her.

Superhero, operating true to form. Melissa almost felt bad for taking advantage of him.

Almost.

"I don't know. I think it's my ankle." She struggled to a halting stand, letting him kneel to palpate her ankle while she put most of her weight on her other foot.

"Can you put your weight on it?"

"I don't know. Let me see."

She shoved off.

"Yeah! I can!" she shouted, the wind tearing her words and laughter off into the light breeze.

She heard him roar, then the pound of his footfalls tearing after her.

She was just close enough to reach the camp before he could overtake her again. She dived, sliding home like a ballplayer scoring the tie-breaking homer of the last game in a World Series.

"I win!" she crowed, but anything else she might have said was walloped out of her when he slid in right behind her, his long, lean legs straddling her body in an intimate fashion that robbed her of what little breath she had left.

Before she could say, "Back off, you big dumb jerk," he'd flipped her.

His eyes glinted dangerously and he was unnervingly close, trapping her beneath his powerful body. Her chest rose and fell harshly, her pulse nowhere close to slowing down.

"Cheaters never prosper," he promised.

"So they say," she answered, helpless.

They stared at each other, inches apart, for long seconds.

His mouth curled dangerously. He was adorable when he smiled. Truly, truly adorable.

"So, really, since you cheated, I won," he pointed out. "Do I get a prize?"

She shook her head even as her arms found a treacherous path up over his shoulders, looping against her will around his neck.

Somewhere along the way, she'd grievously miscalculated. She'd thought expending energy would get rid of it.

Instead, it had made *more* energy.

Her pulse stormed in her ears. A craziness was taking possession of her, and she didn't know if she could contain it.

Especially since the craziness seemed to have taken possesssion of Brade, too. He wasn't doing anything to stop what was happening.

And heaven help her, neither was she.

She imagined herself as a contestant on one of those silly game shows where they asked embarrassing questions like, *Where is the most outrageous place you've ever had sex?*

And she knew without a shred of doubt what her answer would be from this day forward.

On the beach, in broad daylight, on a deserted island in the Atlantic.

"You remember asking me if I'd lost my mind?" Brade murmured huskily.

"Yeah," she whispered.

"It's gone now," he said. "Without a trace. Vanished."

"Mine, too," she breathed right before his mouth came down over hers.

Chapter Thirteen

"We should talk about this," Brade said when he could speak again.

He could feel his own harsh intakes of breath, his own shudder of response as he felt her nipples harden against him through the thin cotton material of her T-shirt.

"I don't want to talk," she whispered.

Her arms were around him, and he felt the new, yet already-familiar lines of her warm body. He was drowning, smothering in her—yet she was breathing life back into him at the same time.

He didn't understand it, just knew this was more than lust. Much more. He didn't want to face what that something more was, and he realized he didn't want to talk about it any more than she did.

She moved slightly, and he found himself pressed even more intimately against her, his hardness fitting to her softness. He felt her heat, even through the clothes that separated them. Her thick blond hair spread out in a tumultuous array around her face, and her eyes gazed back at him, huge and heavy-lidded and wild.

His mouth captured hers with a kiss that was rough and hot. His hands streaked over her, causing her flesh to tremble.

She arched beneath him, breathed his name.

He was going to make love to her. Here, now. He desired her, and he had no doubt that she desired him, too. He was terrified of how much.

There was an inner dam of control that was about to break, and he had no idea what would happen if it did. They had to talk, whether he wanted to or not.

"We shouldn't do this," he said roughly, but she shook her head.

"We should," Melissa whispered, her own voice just as rough. "Don't you feel it? There's something between us, and it's crazy, I know that. But I've never felt anything like it before. I want to make love to you. Now. Today. Because somehow, not making love to you seems even crazier."

Her words sank in with another bolt of searing desire, almost uncontrollable this time. Her touch was like magic, taking him far away from the pain and darkness that had been with him for so long.

He wanted to kiss her into oblivion, bury himself in her soft, warm body and make love to her for the rest of the day.

But he couldn't, not yet.

Not without the truth.

"You're talking about today," he grated, his pulse pounding in his ears, brutal honesty driving him. He cared about her. Too much. Whatever else there was—or was not—between them, he knew there had to be truth. "What about tomorrow?"

He wasn't ready to give her tomorrow. Or forever. Melissa knew that. She didn't know why, didn't know what terrible pain haunted him, but she wasn't going to fight it now. She might lose him, but she wasn't going to lose today.

Today was too precious not to seize and savor for all it was worth.

Tomorrow she would summon the strength to face whatever came. She needed him with an intensity that scared her, but she wasn't going to run from it. She was too drawn at the same time—to his unexpected kindnesses, his gritty vulnerability, his aching darkness.

Without even trying, he reached her on a soul-deep level. Combine that with this kind of desire, and there was no way she was walking away.

Not till she had to.

She wrapped her arms around his neck more tightly and pulled him closer.

"Forget tomorrow," she whispered huskily. "This is today."

"I don't want you to regret—"

She devoured his words with her mouth. "I won't," she breathed when she released him again.

They stared at each other for a moment. He tried to speak, but his voice came out as a growl, and he covered her mouth again in the fiercest of kisses before picking her up and taking her to heaven.

They started in the waterfall. Brade stripped her, one piece of clothing at a time, and she ripped his shirt over his head, his shorts down his legs. It was hot and hungry, wet and wild, and she didn't care because he was laughing and kissing her at the same time, until she pulled away, breathless.

"Wait!" she cried suddenly.

He blinked. "What?"

"I haven't gotten a chance to look at you." She wanted to savor every second, to create a mental photo album that she could take with her.

But her head already felt effervescent, as if she'd drunk her fill of fine champagne.

A laugh curled his hard mouth.

"Okay, you have five seconds," he said teasingly,

but his voice rose lightly in pitch. "After that, I might spontaneously combust if we don't move on."

Melissa started to laugh with him, but her breath caught—not once, but twice, as she lowered her gaze and really looked at him for the first time, taking in every magnificent inch.

And there were a lot of inches.

Superhero inches.

Superhero *hard* inches. And when she lifted her gaze, she found him staring straight at her. His aqua eyes glinted, and she was very aware of her own nakedness but not ashamed.

She'd never felt so openly, unabashedly sexual. She—a virgin!—was dauntless, fearless, bold.

He made her feel so needy and yet so strong at the same time. She didn't understand any of it but it made her love him.

She pushed the realization away, knowing it would spoil the moment.

"Don't rush me," she finally managed cheekily even while her bones melted like butter in a frying pan—with the heat on high.

"I haven't had sex in five years, sweetheart," he told her with a startling honesty that gripped her. "I'll try not to rush, but I can't make any promises."

She swallowed thickly, the impact of his admission sharp in the erotic haze. She doubted he hadn't had sex in five years out of lack of opportunity, and he'd chosen to end his self-imposed celibacy with *her,* for some unknown reason.

Her heart suddenly felt too big to fit into her chest.

"I've never had sex at all," she said, knowing he would realize this for himself soon enough, and knowing that she owed him honesty in return.

He looked stricken. "Sweetheart—"

"No," she demanded, pressing her finger against his mouth. "I want this. I want you. Don't you dare try to deny me now."

His smile returned. "Wow. A dominatrix. Are you sure you're a beginner?"

She laughed back, getting that champagne feeling again. "Just do what I say, big guy, and you won't get hurt."

"Okay," he growled, moving in to nip at her neck.

She moaned with an anticipation that came from deep instinct.

"Tell me what to do . . ." He began to pleasure her, sliding his hands over her, touching her in places she'd never let a man touch her before.

He parted her legs, rubbing her, slipping his fingers inside her, and she gasped.

"Oh, just . . . carry on," she begged in shocked delight, half-laughing, half-panting as his greedy lips found her nape.

He murmured how good she felt, how perfect, all the while his skillful touch ignited a sweet frenzy inside her. Tenderly yet demandingly, he introduced her to erotic sensations she'd only dreamed about before and she swayed against him as he withdrew, and re-entered, again and again—each time finding that small, engorged center.

It was almost impossibly stimulating and finally she had to move, had to respond, driven by urgency and an innate desire to hold back, to draw out this delicious torment—and to share it at the same time.

She reached for him, for that very hard, very large part of him that she knew exactly what to do with despite her complete inexperience. Her heart thudded, and intuition took over as she gripped him.

The groan he released seemed part anguish, part pleasure, and she pressed her mouth to his, swallowing the sound as their mutual need intensified.

Brade's lips opened to her, engaging in a slow dance of tongues as their hands moved over each other, exploring every inch of quivering flesh until she couldn't take it anymore. She didn't know if he picked her up, or if she dragged him down.

She just knew suddenly they were on the soft, mossy bank, their legs and arms tangled, breathless, laughing, kissing.

Then a moment of silence as both of them, drenched, lay together in the sweetness of the shadowed moss and stared at each other.

No words now as they touched again, as he lowered his mouth, kissed her and began to caress her again. Craving him with every fiber of her being, she hugged her thighs around his powerful back and drew him tighter, until he gently forced inside her.

His gaze held hers, watching her carefully, and a

cry slipped out of her—of pain, and then pleasure. She held onto his shoulders and back for dear life, not letting him pull away.

He gave her body a minute to absorb the impact of him. Melissa pushed back, drawing him deeper, closer, needing, wanting. . . .

Slowly, he began to rock and her fingernails dug into his back but still she didn't let go. When she gasped, he crushed his mouth to hers and she tasted all the molten power that he was holding back.

He was trying so hard not to hurt her, not to rush!

"Don't hold back," she pleaded softly, imprisoning him against that pulsing, desperate part of her, clutching her legs more tightly around his body as she rocked against him. "You don't have to hold back anymore," she half-whispered, half-moaned.

His moan mixed with hers, then there was no more holding back, no more restraint.

She didn't want to slow down any more than he did. She needed this—needed *him*—too much to slow down. His kiss turned abruptly frantic as the intensity of his lovemaking turned white-hot.

Pleasure burned through her, and she felt the first rolling shudder of something tumultuous and wonderful when he pulled out of her completely, pushing his hand between them again.

Melissa gasped, trying to yell at him but she couldn't form words. Then she really lost it when she realized *why* he'd put his hand back down there.

Fisting her fingers in his hair, she anchored herself

to the only other person who existed in her entire universe at the moment. His relentless fingers tugged and flicked. Layer after layer of pure pleasure built inside her, shattered, and built again.

It went on and on, and then Brade was back, harder than ever, pushing his arousal even deeper.

He thrust into her wildly and she knew he was as out of control as she was, his eyes filled with intensity and more emotion than she was prepared for.

The incredible sweetness of that instant ripped through her.

And then it was all speed and heat and Brade. He clung to her as if he might die without her, and they cried out a final release together.

Still joined to her seconds later, he brushed back the damp tendrils from her face, both of them breathless and weak. He dropped amazingly tender kisses on her mouth, her nose, her eyelids, and she savored every one.

This was today, Melissa reminded herself silently, and she would live every second of it.

They washed each other with delicious intimacy in the waterfall, and they made love again. Brade speared fish for dinner, and they made love again. She asked him to point out every constellation in the midnight sky, and then they made love one more time.

They never talked about tomorrow again. It was as

if they had a tacit understanding that doing so would break the spell.

It was late before Melissa permitted herself one thought of reality. Whether they spoke of it or not, tomorrow was coming. She had to be prepared.

She had to protect herself.

"I still hate you, you know," she whispered as he zipped up the netting of his tent and lay down beside her, snuggling her sensually aching body against him.

"I hate you, too," he whispered gently back, brushing away the hair at her nape to place a sweet, warm kiss there.

Melissa squeezed her eyes tight in the blackness of the tent and pretended to herself that she wasn't crying.

Chapter Fourteen

They touched down in Charleston at nine forty-five A.M.

Coop and his new bride would be away on their honeymoon by now, or so Brade assumed. Not that he cared at the moment. He just knew he couldn't have spent another moment on Half Moon with Dagmar.

He'd woken up this morning and looked at the breathtaking woman in his arms, and he'd known exactly how she'd felt about planes. His windpipe had tightened, cutting off air. He'd been aroused and stunned and terrified all at once.

His feelings for her went deeper, far deeper, than

he'd ever dreamed possible. She'd changed everything, brought him back to life with startling abruptness.

He felt raw and scared, and he had no idea what to say to her. Luckily, when she'd woken up, she hadn't want to talk.

She'd been distant, and nervous, and he hadn't known what to make of her.

"Take me home," was how she'd greeted him when she came back from the waterfall, showered and dressed in her suit again, and talking in that brittle tone that he knew far too well.

They could have had a few more hours together, but she was already as good as gone from his life. And did he really want it to be any different?

Better to take her back to Charleston, now, before he did something crazy, like beg her to stay with him on Half Moon forever.

But there were some things in life you didn't get twice. He'd had his shot at forever, and it hadn't worked out.

He didn't know if he could handle a second shot. The next one might kill him.

Besides, she was still in love with Coop, wasn't she? That was what this whole weekend had been about to start with—Dagmar's relentless and unwelcome pursuit of his best friend.

So she'd slept with him and she'd never slept with Coop. So she didn't act like a woman in love with another man.

He couldn't figure her out, but what did that mean? He couldn't figure out his own feelings and actions right now, either.

The plane taxied to a stop. He glanced at the woman seated next to him.

The awkward silence was hard to break. He'd give anything for just one of her stinging jabs now. Her silence was worse.

"I'll drive you home," he offered.

She shook her head, avoiding eye contact.

"Not necessary," she said. She fiddled with the handle of her briefcase, but didn't get out of the plane.

He didn't get out, either.

"You came in a cab," he pointed out, annoyed that nothing was ever simple when it came to Dagmar, and annoyed because he wasn't sure if he cared about how she got home . . . or if he just didn't want to let her go.

She met his gaze then. Her eyes were hot, but he could have sworn that the same writhing pain he felt was mirrored there.

His heart tripped, but he felt powerless to do anything—for her, or himself.

They weren't meant to be, he and Dagmar. This weekend was an accident of fate, not a begining of forever.

"That's right, I came in a cab—and I'll leave in a cab, too," she said finally. "I'm not your hostage anymore. Your responsibility ends here. I can take care of myself."

She pushed open the door.

He should get out, he thought to himself. He should go around the plane, help her out. That would be the gentlemanly thing to do.

Only Brade didn't want her to go, and something inside him revolted against the idea of helping her do it. Yet he couldn't stop her, either.

He watched her climb out of his plane, out of his life. She walked across the tarmac to the airfield building. He made himself watch every step, even while his heart nearly broke.

Melissa didn't know what to do first when she got home to the apartment on the second floor of the building that housed Carolina Chic: eat the entire bag of chocolate sandwich cookies in her pantry, take a hot shower, or bury herself in her bed and cry.

Finally, she settled for crying and showering at the same time, and eating the cookies in bed afterward.

So it was the middle of the day and she had nothing on but a towel, her tears, and cookie crumbs. Nobody was there to care, and she deserved a good wallow.

Walking away from Brade had been the hardest, bravest, most grown-up thing she'd ever done. After all, she'd really wanted to throw herself at his feet and beg him to take her back to Half Moon, back to the waterfall. Back to his arms.

But what would that accomplish, besides humiliating her? As much as her heart wanted to fantasize that Brade was a much less troubled man, a man ready to care for her the way she cared for him—her brain wouldn't let her get away with it.

She didn't know what haunted him, and she probably never would. It had to be enough that they'd had their one day. She'd changed, and he was responsible for that. She wasn't afraid of flying anymore. And she wasn't afraid of relationships anymore, either.

Next time, she just had to find the right man to have a relationship with. A man who actually wanted one.

And then she was back to crying again, and the cookie she was holding got soggy, so she put it down and brushed angrily at her cheeks.

She had to stop this. She crumpled up the cookie bag. Crying wasn't going to solve her problems, and the only thing the cookies would do was put back on the couple of pounds she'd lost over the weekend.

Her car wasn't parked behind the building, and there was no sign of Dagmar. They shared the apartment over their office. She'd checked Dagmar's room when she'd come in—the bed was unmade, the room messy.

It was impossible to tell when Dagmar had last been in the apartment—though there were still phone messages on the machine from Friday, and the mail hadn't been brought in since then, either. There was simply a note tacked to the fridge with a magnet, which read, *Sorry about the car—I'll be back in a few days, I promise.*

No telling what tangent had drawn Dagmar away on Friday. Maybe Coop's final rejection had thrown her for such a loop that she'd headed out of town to recover. There was no telling with Dagmar sometimes. Melissa just knew that her erratic cousin was going to get a piece of her mind when she found her.

She forced herself to work up the annoyance she should feel at the pickle Dagmar's behavior over the past weeks had placed her in. It was Dagmar's fault she'd been kidnapped by Brade, after all.

But she couldn't work up any energy to yell at Dagmar for the weekend's events. She couldn't work up any interest in reporting the incident to the police, either—despite all her threats to Brade over the past two days. The only part of her that had really gotten hurt had been her heart—and that was her own fault.

It was Sunday and Carolina Chic wasn't open, but she had to do something or she was going to go straight back to wallowing—and she was sick of herself already.

Balancing the books was as good a way to get her mind off her troubles as any.

She dressed in jeans and a tie-dye T-shirt before heading down the exterior stairs at the rear of the building, flicking on the lights in the office as she entered. She didn't feel like the same person who'd left it on Friday.

Melissa blinked back stupid tears. She stopped at her desk and pulled out the ledger sheets from the file basket. Opening her drawer, she grabbed an armful of folders before going back up the stairs. She took everything out to the tiny back patio at the top of the stairs in front of their door. A brightly striped awning provided shade.

Outside, it was a bright summer afternoon. The building they rented was downtown—and more expensive than they should have dared this early in their business operations. But it came with the apartment, which they'd moved into promptly. Melissa loved the pulse and beat of the historic downtown, and Dagmar was drawn to its incredible ambience and architecture.

Their building was on the corner, and on Sundays the sidewalks around them were always alive with tourists, and Melissa loved people-watching. She tried to focus on the books, but the noisy tourist traffic drew her gaze from time to time. After a while, she went across the street to the deli to get an avocado sandwich, and ate the first nutritious thing she'd had since her return to the real world.

Then she did books and people-watched, and wondered when Dagmar would be back and when she would be able to stop thinking about Brade.

She barely noticed the sound of footfalls coming up the stairs over the general ruckus from the street and inside her mind.

Dagmar, she thought. *Finally.*

Dumping the papers on the patio chair, she leaned over the railing.

"Hey, it's about ti—" Her words jammed in her throat when she realized it wasn't Dagmar coming up.

The achingly familiar face that turned up at her voice wasn't Dagmar's at all.

He cleaned up good, was all she could think in her stunned condition. Her superhero barbarian was wearing what her style sense told her was an expensive brand of casual slacks, a designer short-sleeved knit sports shirt, luxury leather shoes and if she wasn't mistaken, this year's most expensive men's cologne.

She took it all in dazedly, her heart pounding. How could he be such a stranger, and yet be breaking her heart at the same time?

"Hello," he said, adding after a tense beat, "Melissa."

Chapter Fifteen

Melissa worked to steady her breathing. *Be cool,* she warned herself, even as heated awareness streaked through her. She was a mature, independent woman, not a lovesick fool.

She didn't know why Brade was here, but she wasn't going to make it easy for him.

After all, it wasn't easy for her . . . since she was a lovesick fool.

She loved him. She knew that now. She completely and totally loved him. Seeing him again shot that truth home.

But he didn't love her—or if he did, it didn't matter. It had been clear to her on Half Moon that Brade wasn't ready to open up to her, and probably not to anyone.

She had no idea if he'd ever be ready, so she accepted the fact that they weren't meant to be. She couldn't heal whatever wounds were inside Brade— only he could do that.

He had no business showing up here, undoing her with just the sound of her own, real name rolling off his sexy tongue. . . .

"Melissa?" he repeated, taking a step closer.

Her stomach quivered.

Being cool was hard work. But she wasn't a wimp. She was up to the task.

With studied frostiness, she looked to her left, then back to her right, then straight ahead at Brade again.

"Who are you talking to?" she deadpanned. "Can't be me."

Something flickered in his eyes, some emotion she couldn't quite catch.

"I'm sorry," he said quietly. "You were telling me the truth all along, and I didn't believe you."

"Is that what you came here for? To tell me that you're sorry?"

"No." He took a step closer as he spoke.

The porch was small to begin with, and it felt minuscule now. He filled the space with his devastating maleness. She wanted to step back, but there was nowhere to go unless she were to climb on top of her chair.

"And yes," he went on, then stopped, frowned. "I came here because—" He stopped again.

He was . . . flustered, she realized with a slight sense shock.

The superhero was sweetly, nervously, flustered. Had she done that to him? Did he feel as discombobulated as she did? He looked so adorable, she wanted to melt.

She steeled herself to be ice-cold. She was *not* supposed to be melting!

"Why are you here?" she demanded again, folding her arms across her chest tightly and making herself glare at him.

"I did want to apologize," he said finally, and he reached out, touched her shoulders. "And there's something I need to tell you . . ."

Melissa had no idea what he was talking about, but she was going to scream from impatience if he didn't hurry up.

She parted her lips to do just that, but he kissed her first.

He kissed her swiftly, fiercely. Brade had never lost control this way before. He knew that, but he couldn't stop. He didn't want to stop.

He wanted to kiss Melissa for the rest of his life, although he hadn't come here to kiss her. Hell, at the moment he couldn't remember why he had come here.

He *was* kissing her, and that was all that mattered. When he'd seen her, peeking her pretty head over the railing, it'd been all he could do not to bound the rest of the way up the stairs, throw her over his shoulder and haul her off to his cave like some barbarian.

Holding her, he felt pure exhilaration bubbling up inside him. When had he ever felt this unconditionally happy?

Not for a long, long time—if ever, he realized.

How could just being with her make him this happy?

The feeling blew him away. What did it mean? He broke the kiss.

She stared back at him, swaying, and he realized she was blown away, too. He'd undone her that much, just by kissing her.

And dammit, that made him that much happier! It was too much happiness all at once. He didn't know how to deal with it.

He dropped his hold on her shoulders, needing to break the contact for his own sanity, and she tipped back slightly, clutching at the iron tabletop behind her for support.

From the periphery of his vision, he could see the bustle of foot traffic on the sidewalks, hear the cacophony of life in the downtown district.

But it was distant, as far away as if they were still on Half Moon.

"Who," she asked breathlessly, "are you?"

He laughed softly. "Your worst nightmare?"

Melissa laughed back, feeling as shaky as he

sounded. Damn him, how dare he walk into her life, kiss her, make her laugh!

She needed to hate him—but he was making it so hard.

"Yes," she agreed, searching for a foothold in reality, because slipping away into a fantasy world where she and Brade had a chance together was way too tempting and dangerous. They weren't on Half Moon anymore, and it was time for facts, not kisses. "That and—? I don't even know who you are."

The hard lines of his face gentled somehow. "Oh, you know me," he said quietly.

Her breath caught at the intensity of his regard, then shook herself mentally. She had to be tough! Cool!

"You can't just walk in here and kiss me," she pointed out. "We haven't even been properly introduced," she added, managing to sound silly and prim, but she didn't care. At least she didn't sound all hot and melted anymore, which she still was.

His hard lips curved again. He touched her face, his hand drawing a delicate, electric line across her jaw before dropping to his side.

"No, we were never properly introduced," he agreed, and nodded. He stuck out his hand. "Brade Cox."

She bit her lip for a second, hesitant, not sure where this conversation was going and whether she wanted to find out. "Melissa Reynolds," she said finally, shaking his hand.

Mistake! More electric zings zipped up her arm.

She dropped his hand quickly, remembering something.

"Cox?" she repeated. "You're not Leander Cox's private pilot. You're—"

"His grandson."

She couldn't believe it. "You make toys for a living?"

He laughed again, and it struck her that in all the time they'd been on Half Moon, she'd never see him so happy. What was going on?

"That's right," he said. "I make toys. Or rather, I manage the people who makes the toys. I don't exactly make the toys myself. We have employees who do that."

Yeah, like a million of them, she thought dazedly. Her island superhero came from one of the wealthiest, oldest families in South Carolina.

"You're rich," she said.

He nodded. "Does that make a difference to you?"

She thought about it for a second, then shook her head. "No," she answered. "I still hate you."

His intense eyes flickered, and she had the odd feeling she'd said the right thing, though she hadn't been trying to say anything except the truth. She did hate him. Or at least, she wished she did.

"Good." Brade reached out, took her hand again and squeezed it gently. "I'm not sure how I'd feel if anything had changed between us."

"What? In the last six hours, you mean?" she

charged, bewildered about what was happening, still uncertain why he'd come. "Why are you here?" she demanded again.

"Coop," he said. "He's gone."

"Okay," she said slowly, shifting gears. "So what? He's supposed to be gone. On his honeymoon. With his bride. What's the problem?"

"He's not on his honeymoon, or with his bride."

He didn't have to finish. Melissa knew what he was going to tell her, and realized that if she hadn't been so distraught when she'd arrived home, she would have suspected the truth herself.

"Dagmar," she breathed.

He nodded grimly. "It gets worse."

"What do you mean, worse?"

"She kidnapped him."

Melissa stared at Brade for a long beat. "Dagmar couldn't kidnap a flea," was all she could think of to say.

Brade reached into his pocket and pulled out a folded note.

Melissa opened it with shaking fingers. *Don't worry, he'll be okay when the sleeping pill wears off. I'll bring him back in a few days. D.*

Oh, my God. The words formed in her mind but never made it out of her mouth. Dagmar had lost it, well and truly lost it.

Somehow, her cousin had gotten Coop into her car—Melissa's car!—given him a sleeping pill, and carted him off to who knows where. . . .

No wonder Dagmar hadn't had time to wonder where Melissa was all weekend!

"When did this happen?" she managed, trying to concentrate.

"Friday night," Brade explained. "Apparently, he had a a huge fight with Cara—his bride. She had gone over to his condominium and found Dagmar climbing up a ladder to his bedroom window."

Melissa blinked, trying to imagine Dagmar, a ladder, and Coop's bedroom window—

Had the entire world gone insane this weekend? Or at least, her corner of it?

"By the time Cara got to the door, Dagmar was inside, and they had an argument when Coop wouldn't toss Dagmar out. According to Coop's parents, Cara believed Coop was still in love with Dagmar—and the next thing everyone knew, the wedding was called off.

"His parents were hoping Coop and Cara would cool down by Saturday morning," Brade went on, "but by then, Cara was on a plane back to Atlanta, where she's from, and Coop had disappeared. They found the note on Saturday, and were about to call the police—"

Melissa gasped, covered her mouth with shaking fingers as Brade continued.

"—when the phone rang. It was Coop. He said he was all right, told them not to worry, and hung up. But this isn't like him. You have to understand— Coop is the most straightlaced guy you could hope to meet. He doesn't make plans casually—especially wedding plans. He's not the type of guy to break up the night before his wedding and disappear with another woman.

"Coop's the kind of guy who'd be on that next plane to Atlanta, fixing things with Cara," he went on. "When I got in, his parents called me."

He stopped. "That's when I realized—"

He didn't have to explain. Melissa understood. If Dagmar was with Coop, then Dagmar couldn't have been on the island. That's when he'd realized he'd been with Melissa.

"His parents are concerned—" Brade continued.

"And they want you to find him," Melissa finished for him dully. "Make sure he's all right. That's why you're here."

The knowledge was a leaden weight in her chest, tearing down the ridiculous hope she hadn't even realized she'd been cherishing.

"And you want me to help you," she added.

He nodded. "Will you?"

Melissa racked her brain, trying to think where Dagmar could have taken Coop, and working just as hard not to think about how depressing it was that Brade hadn't come rushing over here for the sole purpose of kissing her.

What was wrong with her? She'd actually started hoping that he was here, for her. That he couldn't live without her. That they were about to conduct a scene straight out of the movies where the hero came rushing back to the love of his life. . . .

She sighed. "Sure," she said finally.

"Thank you."

His eyes were warm, and yet unreadable.

She forced herself to turn, pack up her folders. She couldn't stand to keep looking at him.

They'd better find Dagmar fast, she thought desperately.

Then she would make sure she never saw Brade again. She'd move to Mars if she had to. She couldn't take this for long.

It was simply too painful.

"Do you have any idea where we should start looking?" he prodded.

She tucked the files under her arm, still avoiding looking at him directly, and tried to think about where Dagmar could be.

"The cabin!" she cried after a few seconds, daring a peek at his face as she reminded herself to stay tough. No melting!

"What cabin?"

"Her parents had a cabin. A summer place at Lake Marion. We used to go there all the time when we were kids, and it belongs to Dagmar now." Memories rushed back. "I don't know if she'd go there, though," she added, thinking better of the idea.

"Why not?"

"There's no electricity, no running water. Dagmar

would never willingly put herself in those circumstances. She'd have to be nuts—"

She broke off and looked at Brade.

"Let's go," he said.

Chapter Sixteen

Melissa's car was parked in front of the cabin.

"What do we do now?" she asked Brade, wondering if walking in and braining Dagmar over the head with her purse was an option.

It had taken a little over an hour to get there. Melissa had worried halfway that she wouldn't even remember how to get there. She hadn't been to Lake Marion since she was fourteen.

The sun burned low, casting long striped shadows from the pine trees that surrounded the small cabin. Beyond, the lake shimmered in the dying light.

The place hadn't been a palace to start with, and after years of neglect, it looked like a shack.

She couldn't believe Dagmar had really spent the weekend in there, under those primitive conditions.

Then she thought about Half Moon. Talk about primitive conditions. And in the end, she hadn't minded a bit.

She looked at Brade. He pushed open the driver's door of the plush vehicle he'd driven her there in.

"We go up to the door and knock on it," he said sensibly. He cocked a brow. "You got a better idea?"

"I don't know," she said, irritated with him on general principle. "You're the superhero. I thought you might want to find a phone booth first and don your cape."

He grinned, leaned in and kissed her swiftly. "You make me laugh," he said huskily. "That's why I like you so much."

Melissa's heart slammed to a breathless stop. Then she told herself not to be an idiot. So he liked her. Big deal.

"Well, don't get used to it," she said tautly. "After this, you're taking me home. And there's no reason for us to ever see each other again."

She swallowed thickly when she'd finished, and gave him a good glare that felt a little watery. Even that made her mad so she pushed her door open and got out.

"When this is over," Brade said, meeting up with her as she came around the front of the car, "we're going to talk."

Melissa shrugged. Whatever. She wasn't going to

get excited. Talking on the way up to Lake Marion had consisted of depressing banalities. He'd questioned her about Carolina Chic, and she'd responded with questions about Cox Toys.

They could have been two businesspeople meeting for the first time at a cocktail party for all the depth the conversation had held.

Brade rapped sharply on the decrepit wood door to the cabin. Melissa was amazed it didn't simply fall in.

There was the sound of laughter, a shriek, and then a thud from inside, followed by more laughing.

She looked at Brade.

"Maybe we should—" she started to say, but stopped short when the door swung open.

A man stood there, naked from the waist up—and not wearing anything more than a wrapped sheet below that. He had big shoulders and chest muscles—and Dagmar, clinging onto his back, her bare feet locked around his waist from behind.

"Hi, Melissa!"

Dagmar beamed at Melissa from over Coop's—surely it was Coop, unless she'd kidnapped another man, too?—shoulder, and Melissa had a sinking feeling that her cousin and Coop were sharing that sheet.

"Coop?" Brade asked. Melissa noticed he looked as stunned as she felt.

Coop wore the most sloppy, silly grin Melissa had ever seen.

"What are you doing here?" Coop began, then

nodded knowingly. "My parents." Dagmar slipped a little, giggled, and Coop reached back with one hand, holding onto the sheet with the other. Melissa heard a gentle slap and realized she was right—Dagmar was naked back there. Coop was slapping her bottom! Coop focused on Brade again. "My parents must have sent you."

Dagmar was slipping down Coop's back again. Melissa skirted around the two of them, grabbed a blanket off the bed in the corner of the one-room cabin and threw it at her cousin, trying not to look as Dagmar straightened herself. She was afraid Coop's behind might be as bare as Dagmar's.

Melissa took in the rest of the cabin in a blur. There were candles burning everywhere, and the place did look romantic, she had to admit. Dagmar must have planned it, she realized abruptly. This was no spur-of-the-moment escapade. The old cabin was clean, filled with fresh flowers and potpourri. There were plates stacked on each side of the bed, and glasses, and a cooler in the kitchen area.

From the look of things, she doubted Dagmar and Coop had been anywhere but in bed most of the weekend, though.

"Your parents were worried," Brade explained.

Coop nodded, serious suddenly. "I've already apologized to them on the phone," he said. "But I'm going to do it again, as soon as I get back to Charleston. And I owe you an apology, too—I never should have asked you to get Dagmar out of the way."

He turned, put his arm around Dagmar and squeezed her close. "Thank God you didn't do it," Coop said.

Melissa felt Brade's eyes turn to her, and she worked hard to ignore him.

"And thank God Dagmar didn't give up on us," Coop went on, still serious. "I love her, Brade. I loved her all along—but my parents were against the marriage. They don't know Dagmar. They think she's kooky."

Dagmar smiled proudly.

"But she's not!" Coop defended. "She's just interesting. Aren't you, sweetie?"

Dagmar nodded and nestled closer.

"I have to admit, I was a fool," Coop said. "My parents wanted me to marry Cara ever since we were kids. Same with Cara's parents. And we tried, we really did. We both wanted to do the right thing—but the right thing was wrong this time. Cara made me see it. As much as I love my parents, I love Dagmar—not Cara, and they're going to have to accept her. Cara doesn't love me, either, and I think she was pretty grateful we both saw the light in time."

Coop shook his head. "She told me that she's in love with her tennis coach. They're probably in Vegas now, getting married."

He shot a look at Dagmar. "Which might be where we're headed next."

Melissa had never seen Dagmar happier. She felt

a tight, hot knot in her stomach, and realized with horror that it was jealousy.

She reached out, put her arms around Dagmar.

"I'm so happy for you," she whispered. "And I'm going to kill you when you get back!"

Dagmar laughed. "I'm sorry for causing so much trouble."

"You don't know the half of it . . . yet," Melissa promised her.

"I almost missed the love of my life," Coop said. He squeezed Dagmar close again. "Almost." He kissed her, and the sheet started slipping off his waist and Dagmar's blanket did a dive.

Brade pulled the cabin door shut behind them as he and Melissa stepped outside. They stood on the stoop in the dying light, with more sounds of laughing and shrieking and thudding filtering from inside the cabin again.

The jealousy had abated, and now Melissa felt numb. Empty. It was time to go home, never to see Brade again.

He cared about her, she believed that—even if he hadn't exactly said so. But she needed more than that. "Well," Brade said.

"I guess that's over," Melissa said sadly.

They drove a mile back down the narrow one-lane road that led to the remote cabin, almost to the highway that would take them to the interstate and Charleston.

Brade pulled over and stopped the car. The sudden silence and stillness was overwhelming. He could hear his heartbeat, and he realized how alive he felt.

The truth had hit hard when he'd listened to Coop's words. The past would always be part of him, but Melissa was his future.

He was still scared of the powerful feelings, scared of losing her someday, just as he'd lost Rebecca. But he wasn't going to let that fear stop him, not anymore.

Like Coop, he'd almost let the best thing that had ever happened to him slip through his fingers.

He took a deep breath.

"Melissa?"

"What?"

"You don't really hate me, do you?"

Brade's question threw Melissa. Why was he making this whole thing so hard? Just being with him was breaking her heart. She wanted to get back to Charleston and be done with it.

He'd told her he liked her, and that was nice, but she didn't want to be friends.

She couldn't look at him, so she gazed at her hands.

"Yes," she said. "I really, really hate you." She felt a big tear well up and she dashed at her eye, but just as soon as she'd vanquished that one, another big tear was welling up in the other.

She pushed the car door open and marched up

the grassy roadside about ten feet and sucked in a few breaths. Being cool was killing her.

"Well, I don't hate you," he said, coming up behind her.

He touched her shoulder, but she didn't turn.

"Actually, I love you," he added.

Melissa's knees almost gave out. She wheeled, her heart climbing right up her throat.

He was standing there, looking so honest and vulnerable and cute.

She wanted to believe him. Or punch him. One of the two.

"How can you be in love with me? We just met on Friday," she pointed out sensibly.

She knew how she could be in love with him, she just couldn't accept that he loved her back. It was too perfect. Perfect stuff didn't happen to Melissa Reynolds.

He reached out, took her hand, tugged her so that she took a helpless step toward him just as he took one toward her.

"I don't know," he admitted, looking adorably, devastatingly, awestruck. "Trust me, I'm as surprised as you are. If you'd asked me last week if I was ever going to fall in love again, I would have told you there wasn't a chance in hell." He shook his head. "But this weekend, you changed everything.

"You pulled me out of that dark well of self-pity I was caught in, and you made me feel alive again. You made me realize there are second chances—even for love.''

Melissa exhaled a long, slow breath. Her heart was pitter-pattering like crazy.

"Tell me about your first chance," she said, knowing that she had to know everything. That she had to be sure he'd put behind him whatever had haunted him for so long.

"I was married, five years ago," he explained. "Rebecca found out she was sick exactly two weeks later. There was nothing they could do—it was an inoperable cancer. She was gone before our first anniversary."

"Oh, Brade," Melissa whispered, her voice trembling with quick emotion. She felt those big tears coming right back, and she didn't try to stop them this time.

His lips brushed hers.

"I thought that was it for me," he went on, still holding her close. "Losing Rebecca hurt so badly. I couldn't save her—there was nothing I could do. I'd never felt so out of control, and I didn't want to feel that way again. Then you came along—and boy, did I ever feel out of control!

"But it was good," he said huskily, kissing her again. "It was more than good. I was killing myself trying to be in control, trying not to let myself feel anything.

"But you just stomped right into my heart and stole it, sweetheart," he said, his gaze open, revealing all his feelings, nothing hidden anymore.

He looked at her with joy and hope and a searing need that rocked her to her core, filling her with a giddy blossom of happiness.

"You wouldn't let me *not* feel. And I'm so grateful for the day I mistook you for Dagmar and hijacked you to Half Moon."

Melissa was crying. And she was laughing. He kissed her, and it was all wet and warm and perfect. Really perfect.

"Maybe we should lobby to have that day made into a national holiday," she said. "Because I'm pretty grateful for it, too." She swallowed thickly, figuring she must look like a sloppy mess, with mascara running down her face. But Brade didn't seem to care. "You changed my life, too," she told him. "The flying—"

"You've been scared of planes for a long time," he guessed.

She nodded.

"I was on a plane with my parents when I was four years old," she told him. "It crashed on landing."

"Sweetheart." He hugged her closer.

"My parents didn't make it," she explained. "I grew up with Dagmar's family. They were good parents, but very distant. I learned to keep to myself, not to expect love. Dagmar didn't receive much more affection than I did." She smiled crookedly. "When you get to know Dagmar, you'll understand her. Coop's right—she's really not kooky—just interesting." Brade lifted a dubious brow, and she laughed. "Okay," she said. "Maybe a little kooky."

"Was that when you started stuttering?" Brade asked, looking at her seriously again. "After the crash?"

She nodded. "It took me years to grow out of it," she told him. "I hadn't relapsed in years, until you threw me for a loop!" she said, and socked him playfully in his hard stomach.

He just hugged her tighter and she pressed her wet cheek against his chest.

"I think I knew, from the beginning, that you could unsettle my safe little world," she whispered. "And all the biggest fears inside me came bursting back— mostly, that I would never be loved."

"I do love you, Melissa. So much."

"I love you, too," she whispered.

And he kissed her again, wrapping his arm around her as if he would never let her go. She shuddered in his arms, giving kiss for kiss, needing him so unbelievably much—and reveling in how much he needed her in return.

"I see a honeymoon on Half Moon," he predicted.

She smiled, snuggling into his chest, feeling more complete and happy than she ever had in her whole life.

"Me, too," she agreed. "But just one thing . . ."

Brade pulled back, arched a probing brow. "What?"

"Well, maybe more than one thing," she explained. "I see a house, too. With a kitchen and lots of cookies, and a bathroom with a really hot shower, and a TV, and a bed—"

"Okay," he said, his hard mouth curving, "as long as I get what I want."

She smiled back at him, feeling bubbly and dizzy and oh so happy inside. "What's that?" she asked.

"You." He held her tightly. "Just you."

ABOUT THE AUTHOR

Suzanne McMinn writes contemporary and historical romances from her small Texas town, accompanied by the clamor of life with three energetic children. To learn more about her books, visit her web site at:

http://www.SuzanneMcMinn.com